Copyright © 2018 by Lovestruck Romance.

All Rights Reserved.
No part of this publication may be reproduced, distributed or transmitted in any form or by any means including photocopying, recording, or other electronic or mechanical methods except in the case of brief quotations embodied in critical reviews and certain other noncommercial uses permitted by copyright law. The unauthorized reproduction or distribution of this copyrighted work is illegal.

This book is a work of fiction. Names, characters, businesses, places, events, and incidents are either the products of the author's imagination or used in a fictitious manner. Any resemblance to actual persons living or dead is purely coincidental.

This book is intended for adult readers only.
Any sexual activity portrayed in these pages occurs between consenting adults over the age of 18 who are not related by blood.

FIRE BREATHING CEZAR

DRAGONS OF THE BAYOU

CANDACE AYERS

LOVESTRUCK ROMANCE

CONTENTS

Story Description   vii

1.	Cherry	1
2.	Cezar	8
3.	Cherry	15
4.	Cezar	23
5.	Cherry	29
6.	Cezar	35
7.	Cherry	40
8.	Cezar	46
9.	Cherry	52
10.	Cezar	59
11.	Cherry	66
12.	Cezar	72
13.	Cherry	78
14.	Cherry	85
15.	Cherry	92
16.	Cezar	99
17.	Cezar	108
18.	Cherry	114
19.	Cezar	122
20.	Cherry	127
21.	Cezar	134
22.	Cherry	139
23.	Cezar	144
	Epilogue	150

Something's Lurking in the swamplands of the Deep South...

Small town librarian Cherry Deschamps is perfectly content with her safe, mundane existence.
Others might consider an evening with a mug of hot cocoa, bowl of Ramen noodles, and a Netflix marathon boring. Not her.

When the panty-meltingly gorgeous "Mr. Hollywood" enters her life showering her with gifts and attention, of course she's skeptical. She's learned from an early age that vulnerability leads to pain and heartache.

Cezar fights his every animalistic instinct to win over his human mate.
He does his best to behave like a human male.
In the end, though, it may take the fierce possessiveness of his dragon to convince his mate she's worthy of love.

This is a feel-good shifter rom-com novella that transports you to a place where laughter is the status quo and a smile on your face is guaranteed.

1

CHERRY

The Carl A. Brasseaux Library, a branch of the Lafourche Parish Public Library system had served as more than just a place of employment for me. It had, for a number of years, been a beacon of hope that had transformed into something more—my home. Between the covers of books, with the scent of paper, ink and adhesive wafting from the pages, I found escape, freedom and even a sense of belonging.

In the big, brick building I had finally reached the goal I'd held since I'd been a lost and unwanted child shuffled through the foster care system. I was the new head librarian. The crotchety spinster that I had replaced, Miss Slair, had been the head librarian for over forty years. She'd been there when I was a kid, just as sour-faced and snarly as she was at her retirement party a few days prior. I'd been waiting for her to retire for so long that I'd nearly jumped for joy when the announcement was made that she was stepping down and I would be replacing her. Not only did that mean I would finally get to escape her reign of terror, but more importantly, it meant fulfilling my dream of moving from part time library aid to full time librarian. Benefits, more money, and two weeks of paid vacation. I had made it.

I realized that most people wouldn't be as over the moon as I was to get a job as librarian in a small branch library in Louisiana bayou country. But, I'd gone to college, gotten my degree in library science, and continued to work part time at the Brasseaux Library, all in eager anticipation of this exact job. This exact day. This exact moment.

I loved books—everything about them. The smell of them, the look of them, the heft of them whether hugged against the chest or carried under the arm. But, what's more, I loved the worlds they unlocked. The alternate realities and the characters who lived lives of adventure, romance, mystery, and intrigue. The moment I stepped through the doors of the place as a girl of almost twelve years old, it changed my life. I still relished the peaceful sounds, the hushed, whispered voices, the pages being flipped, the keyboard keys being struck.

I unlocked the front doors and stepped through them on that chilly Monday morning. I stood for a moment grinning, breathing deeply, and indulging myself in the familiar scents.

What a beautiful morning, I marveled, as I flipped on the lights. A few years back, a good deal of money had been donated to have the old building remodeled on the inside and a local contractor had worked nothing short of a miracle. Everything was new and pristine, large bookshelves made of real wood, hanging pendant lamps throughout, solid oak floors that our fabulous janitor, old Eustace, kept shined to perfection. It was my little slice of heaven and I intended to leave an impression.

"Our first day without The Slayer!" Cameron Davis' raised voice echoed through the main room startling me out of my reverie, sending me stumbling forward and clutching my chest. "Don't we have an old disco ball in the basement from that 70's themed fundraiser we did a few years back? I feel like boogying through the stacks!"

I shot her a look. "Can you not give me a heart attack first? I'd love to experience my first day as head librarian right here rather than spending it in the emergency room of Lafourche General."

"Sorry. I snuck in behind you when I saw you coming in. I kinda wanted to see what you'd do. Slayer always came in and wiped the counters with her boney old knobby fingers to check for dust. She was just waiting for a chance to ream poor Eustace."

"And you were expecting the same from me?" I raised a brow.

"Not at all. You did just what I thought you'd do. You looked around this place like it's the Taj Mahal and it's just been gifted to you." She rolled her eyes. "I've never known anyone's panties to get wet from being in a library."

"Really, Cameron?" I turned away so she didn't see me blush. It was embarrassing that at almost thirty, I was still so prudish that I blushed over silly, carnally-natured comments. The truth was, anything of a sexual nature flustered me but, along with my new job, I had plans to change that.

I was starting to consider it as a thing of shame that at my age I was still a virgin, as though I was too afflicted with repulsiveness or damage to even get a man to sleep with me. It wasn't true—at least I didn't think it was. At any rate, I vowed that this would be the year to remedy that affliction, just to say I did it. Pun intended.

New job, new life, new page.

Maybe in the end I would turn out to be the proverbial old maid spinster librarian like, I shuddered, Miss Slair, but at least I ought to know what I was missing. It would be a choice, not an affliction.

Yep, *new page*.

I glanced at Cameron. "Come on. Since you snuck in early, you can help me get the stuff set up for this morning."

"Your first Kiddie's Corner, huh?"

My first everything—a year of firsts. "I think I'm going to change that name, too." I looked over at where the kids would soon be piled up on the pillows and carpet squares we brought out. Miss Slair had always made them sit in an orderly fashion before she started and would give them nasty, stink-eyed glares if they got too fidgety or excited. "This is going to be fun. What do you think about calling it The New Adventure Zone?"

~

The day passed far too quickly and, by closing time, I still felt full of energy, like I could do it all again right then and there. I loved being free to interact with the children and other visitors who came and went. The big place already felt lighter and more welcoming with Miss Slair gone. The Slayer would not be missed.

"What are you doing to celebrate your first day as the big wig?" Cameron plopped a stack of books down on the circulation desk and grinned at me. "A steamy night of Ramen noodles, hot cocoa, and Netflix?"

"Ha. Ha. Funny."

"You're not disagreeing."

"Well, I'm not agreeing either. Which means maybe it's noodles and chocolate, *or* maybe it's a hot date and a night on the town." It definitely was not a date; it was never, ever a date. In fact, her suggestion of Ramen, cocoa and Netflix sounded pretty good to me, not that I was about to admit it aloud. I was a homebody—an introverted bookworm who adored her boring life. Mostly.

"Yeah, okay." She scooted the books towards me and smiled sweetly. "Well, I *do* have a hot date. Do you mind putting these away for me so I can get out of here?"

I was already nodding before she finished her sentence. We both knew I didn't have anything planned for the evening. Plus, I liked staying late at the library and experiencing the place alone. My morning serenity had been invaded by Cameron, so I'd take some quiet alone time at my home away from home when I could. "Go ahead."

"Thanks! You're a doll." She was almost a blur she got out of there so fast.

I leaned against the desk and took it all in. My life might've been boring and kind of lonely, but I was really proud of myself. I was once just a kid in the system—a kid whose chances of not ending up either in prison, addicted to drugs or dead by the time I'd reached thirty were statistically abysmal. Yet, I'd beaten the odds. Brick by brick, I'd built myself a stable, respectable life. Sure, I didn't venture too far out of my comfort zone. I wasn't a big risk taker. But, who said a life had to be wild and crazy to be valid? A quiet life surrounded by the worlds of adventure between the pages of a good book was all the excitement I needed. It was a life, right?

The oversized clock on the wall above the desk chimed that it was six-thirty. I grabbed the stack of books to shelve. I knew the shelves like the back of my hand, so it took me no time. Then, I made my rounds, making sure everything was put away all neat and tidy. Luckily I was alone because I probably looked like I'd lost my mind since I couldn't wipe the huge grin off my face.

I grabbed my things and scanned the room once more before locking the massive wooden doors and stepping out under the large front awning. The night had already descended, and winter had arrived earlier than expected that year. It was a sweater and bonfire night. Despite my insistence that I loved to be alone, I was still buzzing with excitement about my first day and wanted to share it with someone. Maybe I could persuade Chyna, my twin, to come over for dinner to help me celebrate. I'd even supply the hot cocoa.

I lived within walking distance of the library, and as I headed down the street towards my house, I was overcome with a vaguely empty feeling. It was like a sixth sense that gnawed at my gut, leaving me feeling a bit hollow, like something was missing. It was disappointing considering I'd just finished my first day at my dream job—the goal that I'd been pursuing for over a decade.

A gust of evening chill blew over the quiet street and I shuddered. No, it wasn't just that something was missing; it was that something was coming. I had a strange inkling that something was about to change. I could feel it in my bones like a sixth sense.

Sixth sense, pshaw, I chided myself. I didn't believe in all that 'spirits-and-curses-and-spells' mumbo jumbo that was so prevalent down here in the bayou country of the deep south.

It was probably just that I was letting Cameron's comments get to me. A girl didn't need to go out on the town or have hot dates lined up to enjoy herself. There was nothing inherently empty about a calm, safe life. I was…happy. I was.

I pulled out my phone and dialed my sister. Fortunately, life had blessed me with a twin, someone that made it impossible for me to ever truly be alone. Instead of getting Chyna, however, I got her voicemail. Afraid of my recorded voice sounding needy and pitiful, I hung up without leaving a message. Chyna would be able to pick up on my mood right away, even in a transmission through a cell tower. We had that kind of connection.

As I walked the rest of the way home, I decided that I'd just crawl into bed early with the best bed partner a girl could ever have—the latest release from my favorite cozy mystery author.

2

CEZAR

Dragons tended to be kind of territorial about their homes —castles—what have you. It was innate. I, and the others who'd arrived in the new world along with me, were no different. Only on rare occasions, usually emergencies or crises, did we all gather at one of our castles. Usually, however, we chose a neutral meeting place. Currently, that meeting place was in the middle of secluded swampland on an old abandoned barge.

None of us was sure how long the barge had been there, or when or why it had been abandoned, but our kind had arrived in our new world just a couple decades shy of a century ago, and I, for one, remembered a time when that stretch of swamp was empty. All any of us could say about the matter was that one day there was nothing, the next, a very large abandoned barge.

We always flew in. The weather was cool that night and the flight was pleasant. It felt good to stretch my wings out and have the evening breezes roll over my scales. Yet, I still had a deep, restless feeling, an antsiness. I'd been feeling that way for days. Dragons shouldn't feel antsy. It wasn't safe. No animal the size of a small building should ever feel anything remotely close to antsy.

Armand, Remy, and Blaise were already there when I arrived. Ovide was missing. No surprise. He was never on time. Beast was absent as well, but I didn't expect him. I figured he was far too busy to attend any meetings for a while. Besides, the evening's topic didn't concern him. He'd found his mate. No doubt, he was at home right that moment enjoying his new family. Lucky firemouth. I was happy for him, really, but there still remained a tiny sliver of me that was ragingly jealous. Rarely did I covet another dragon's treasures, but a mate was a treasure unlike any other. Beast had, as the humans saying went, "hit the jackpot". His mate was fantastic and she came with two young males whom I had grown very fond of.

Armand was seated on an old crate, his face expressionless, despite the fact that we all knew the wheels in that dragon's head were always spinning. He was probably thinking about the next batch of brew he was cooking up. Spirits of the new world barely affected us, and then only if we imbibed vast quantities. They were hardly worth it. Armand took it upon himself not only to keep alive the recipes of the old world brews, but to improve upon them creating new ways to get a dragon shit-faced.

"You and Ovide are always late." Remy scowled. "Do you think we like sitting around in the middle of this swamp like crusty old scalywings?"

Blaise rolled his eyes at his twin brother. "Like we have anywhere better to be. We've been sitting around like crusty old scalywings for over seventy-five years now. Besides, I kind of like this place. It's like a secluded island. I used to go to the one that Beast found until he mated all over it. Now, I can't stomach the stench."

I walked the width of the barge and stared out at the wetland. It wasn't so unlike our old world. Most of the time the swamp was pretty similar—hot, muggy, and sometimes containing the rising odor of rot and decay.

"Islands are great." Remy shrugged. "But, mates would be better."

I stood facing my fellow dragons. "He's right. We're not here to admire our surroundings or to find a personal oasis. I think you all know why I have called you here tonight. And, I am certain you'll all agree that we have a grave matter at hand."

There was a collective sigh. I assumed that most of us wanted a mate, although there was at least one of us in the group that got along just fine without a female around. But, our *desire* for mates wasn't the grave matter of which I spoke. It was our *need* for mates. Mates were a necessity for our kind. A male dragon had a certain length of time to find his mate. After that time passed, if he was still without one, he would deteriorate to his most base, animalistic form. Not only that but, like a ticking clock, our time was nearing the end. We'd estimated that those of us who did not find a mate by the lunar eclipse were done for. We would slowly lose our minds and eventually shift into our dragon form to be permanently locked there, unable to ever shift back.

I had not thought that part completely through while instructing my brethren to run as fugitives from our old world. To be fair, it had never been a consideration for our kind before because there had been plenty of females in the old world. The question of whether a male would find a mate before his biological clock ran out had never before been raised.

Then, the slayers had managed to increase their numbers, and their threat to us to the point...well, the best option for our kind had been to seek out a new home. There was much more to the story, but the bottom line was that there we were, the handful of us, as far as we knew the lone survivors of our race, doing the best we could to survive.

If we deteriorated and went full-on crazy dragon on Earth, our dragon brethren would be obliged to put us down. For the sake of the inhabitants of the new world.

"Our time to find mates is quickly running out. Now that Beast has mated Sky, I feel as though we've been given hope, at least." I stopped pacing and looked up at the twinkling stars. "But what we've been doing for the past near-century, which is little more than wait, hasn't been very...efficient."

"But what are we *supposed* to be doing?" Blaise was absently staring into the murky water beside him. He suddenly shook his head at something just under the surface and gave a soft hiss. "Get along, little gator," he whispered, "my teeth are much bigger than yours."

"I've been researching."

Groans went up amongst the males. Even Ovide, who'd just landed with a thud, let out a dragon sized groan. Shifting into his human form, he held out his hands, palm up. "This again?"

"We must find mates, Ovide."

Ovide growled. "I'm out of here. Call me when it's time to get fucked up on Armand's brew."

I went on, ignoring the fact that he instantly shifted back and flew away. "There are a lot of different places human males meet their females."

Remy perked up. "Like where?"

"Bars. Parks. Churches..."

"We're supposed to go to church to find a female?" Shaking his head, Remy blew out a rough breath. "Church? Come on, Cezar."

"I'm just telling you what I've read. Do what you want with the information."

"Where else?"

"Grocery stores, the workplace, various community events such as fairs and festivals..." I wracked my brain for others and came up with only one. "Ah, yes, humans are now dating online as well."

Blaise pulled a face that read all kinds of confused. "On *what* line?"

"*Online*. The internet."

"On the computer? How do you date on a computer?"

I ran a hand through my hair. I wasn't actually sure. I hadn't yet figured that one out. "I'll have to do a little more research on that."

"I don't like any of this. I don't want to have to go out and do human things in the hopes I might find my mate. I have hope she will come to me. Beast's mate showed up on his doorstep. Why can't mine do the same?" Without waiting for a reply, Armand shifted and took off into the air, projecting his thoughts to all of us:

This. Fucking. Sucks.

Remy and Blaise sighed in unison, gave each other side glances, and both took off in flight at the same time. Their red and orange scales lit up the sky like flames as they pumped their powerful wings.

Left alone with my thoughts, I sat on the edge of the barge and dropped my head. I didn't blame them for the attitudes. I, too, felt their desperation. It was almost as though we could all feel the eclipse approaching and our lives nearing a bitter end. It inched towards us like a slow crawling insect creeping up the backs of our necks. We had witnessed the slaughter of our species and the destruction of our kind. Somehow, a loss like that made it too easy to give up. All too easy for the desperation to turn to resignation.

I did not exactly relish the thought of hanging out at a grocery store trying to run into my mate, either, but a dragon had to do what a dragon had to do.

I shifted and took to the sky, a giant green beast. It had been a miracle how we'd kept our existence a secret among humans. I supposed most humans see only what they want to see. And the few who had seen us were dismissed as having lost their marbles. So, to them we existed as mere folklore, like fucking Big Foot or UFOs.

I needed to begin my search. But first, I needed to go home and put clothes on. Humans did not like it if you walked around without clothes. In fact, they arrested you. So, clothes first, then, I'd start the search at the grocery store. I needed to buy stuff for dinner, anyway. I'd found a new recipe I wanted to try. If I did not encounter my mate at the Save-and-Shop, at least I would have a nice meal.

Although some of the other dragons may not have been keen on finding a mate, I was. I couldn't wait to find mine and mount her. I couldn't wait to have younglings running around the castle. But, I also knew that human customs surrounding mating were vastly different than our own. It had been hard work for any of us to fit into the human world. I continued to do my best to research and study their literature and culture to fit in.

On the human mating rituals and customs, I had a good idea what modern humans did and didn't do. I was prepared to try anything and everything the books said. I would rein in my beastly nature and adhere to their customs—do what was necessary to find and procure a mate.

Unfortunately, their customs went so far against my nature at times that they felt daunting.

3

CHERRY

Cameron only worked at the library three days a week. The other two and a half days were worked by an older woman named Marilyn. Marilyn was easier to work with and probably loved the library just as much as I did. Slayer had never let her do any of the readings. I, from personal experience, knew that Marilyn could read a book aloud like nobody's business. She gave life to characters and held even the most distracted listeners' attention. Slayer had wasted Marilyn's talents for years, but I wasn't about to.

The library stayed open late on Fridays for an antiquated book club with such low attendance that it should have been shut down years ago. The only reason it was still allowed to continue under the budget was that it was made up of Slayer and her four friends. I thought about nixing it, but it was ingrained in my nature to encourage reading and to share books. So, I decided that rather than scrap the program, I'd make a few changes and update the club format, try to bring in fresh blood.

Change number one, no more pretending that reading Jane Austen was a hip and trendy thing to do on a Friday night. Don't get me wrong, I could read Jane Austen anytime, Friday nights included, but I wanted to attract a bigger crowd—women who deserved a little "me time" to unwind and let their hair down. We needed to mix it up a little. Which was why I'd given Marilyn free rein to select a book of her choice and read from it. I'd also encouraged her to put up notices around town inviting new people.

Finally allowed the freedom to prove herself, Marilyn had taken the reins and run with them. The turnout far exceeded my expectations. The meeting room was full of younger women mixed in with the few older ones and, despite Slayer doing her best to scare away the newcomers, they looked like they were having a great time. I'd brought in a few bottles of wine and juice and refreshments and the ladies seemed completely satisfied to drink cheap wine out of paper cups while Marilyn read about the intricate difficulties of forming a lasting relationship from a BDSM hook up. Okay, maybe I should have added the stipulation that I need to *approve* the evening's book before I transferred the reins to Marilyn. Who knew she was such a freak?

My face was crimson with embarrassment, but it was worth it to watch Slayer's friends squirming in their seats as Marilyn read words that they'd probably never heard spoken aloud before. Lord knew I hadn't. And Marilyn didn't just read...she performed. The thing was, everyone, except Slayer, seemed to be enjoying themselves. Granted, I was mighty uncomfortable with the whole topic, but I was enjoying the hell out of watching Slayer who looked as though she'd just sucked the pits out of a lemon.

Fire Breathing Cezar 17

At the end of the evening, when everyone had either stumbled home or had their sober partners drive them, I picked up the paper cups and returned the chairs to their proper positions. I'd assumed everyone had already gone, so when Slayer did her signature throat clearing behind me, I jumped straight up into the air about a mile.

"Oh! Sweet baby Jesus, you scared me!" I pressed my hands to my chest and shook my head. "You snuck up on me, Miss. Slair."

"We need to discuss something, Cherry. I wasn't keen on embarrassing you your first week on the job, but I found tonight to be incredibly inappropriate. Alcohol, smut books…I haven't even been gone for a full week yet and already the library is showing signs of becoming a den of iniquity. I'm worried."

I forced a smile. "Don't be. I assure you that everything is going fine."

"Then how do you explain this evening?"

"I don't need to explain, Miss. Slair. We all passed a good time. It was a record turnout and all the attendees left happy. That Marilyn can really bring a story to life, can't she?"

"*Everyone* certainly did not enjoy themselves. The original club members did not expect to come here and listen to… to…pornography."

I inhaled slowly and kept my smile plastered reminding myself that they had stayed, hadn't they? They could have left at any time. "I'm sorry if you didn't like the new direction that the book club is going in. I just want to get a larger group of women involved, bring in more diversity. Women of all ages. I suppose that if we can't agree on content, maybe we can break off into two groups."

"And have those trashy goings on taking place under the same roof?"

"You could move the meetings to your house, if you'd like." My smile was concrete and steel. "Or, you could meet here on Saturday mornings, I suppose."

"That is just ridiculous. I should never have left this place. I should never have retired. It won't be long before this library falls to depravity and ruin." She stormed away from me, her final glare a menacing one. "I'll be speaking to the parish president about this."

I bit back a nasty retort and turned to the circulation desk where Marilyn was conversing with a nice looking guy. When she turned and pointed him in my direction, all thoughts of Slayer fled. I took a step forward and gave the guy a "head librarian" smile. "How can we help you?"

Marilyn grinned at me from just behind him and waggled her brows. "Not we. You. He asked for you. I'll just finish the cleanup here."

I wanted to reach out and grab her arm, but the man was looking down at me with such intensity that I couldn't. "Okay. How can *I* help you, then?"

He smiled a cocky half smile at me and ran his eyes up and down my body, scanning. When he got back to my face, I was sure it was bright red. He was handsome, alright, with bright blue eyes and boyish good looks. "I was hoping to talk to you for a bit. I see you're busy, though."

The crazy notion that he was going to ask me out on a date came over me and I found my hand in my hair, trembling a bit, as I twisted a strand around my finger. I was fighting like a gladiator against the instinct that told me to run. *Stop it! New page, Cherry, new page.* I would never experience my first sexual encounter if I ran every time a man showed any interest in me.

Sexual encounter? That was insane. I was acting insane. I didn't know the man. Did I? I studied his face again. Nope. Never seen him before. Why would he want to ask me out? Although, that was how it worked in romance novels, right? I scanned his face and body again taking another assessment. Would this guy be my first lover? "Um, a little busy, yes. I, um, need to help Marilyn finish cleaning."

Marilyn cleared her throat from not too far away. "I'm going to finish up this little bit by myself. Y'all go ahead. I'll lock up for the night."

I hesitated. "You don't have to do that…"

"Go!" She shot me a stern look and tied up a trash bag. "I'll see you in the morning."

The man smiled down at me. "I'm Taylor, by the way. I'd love to walk you home."

Warning bells sounded in my head. "Um…I don't know…"

"I know your sister. I'm not a creep. I promise." He laughed lightly and shrugged. "Call Chyna."

Marilyn pushed my shoulders, towards Taylor, and scoffed. "Of course you're not a creep. She doesn't need to call Chyna. She'd love it if you walked her home."

I sighed and nodded. "O-kay."

Taylor grinned, boyish charm oozing out of him. "Great. Let's go."

I grabbed my purse from behind the desk and pulled the strap over my shoulder. "I'm ready."

As we headed out of the library and in the direction of my house, I glanced over my shoulder. The glowing lights of the library against the darkening night were pulling me back. I was never comfortable in the presence of men. Ever. Especially not handsome ones who smiled megawatt smiles and asked to walk me home.

I had all kinds of issues—fear of commitment, trust issues, abandonment issues. Hell, what former foster kid could escape issues? I had, however, vowed to turn a new page, which meant I had to summon up more courage. I was fortunate in that, number one, I'd had a few paper cups of wine, and number two, Taylor was too cute to be a psychotic serial killer.

"So, what did you want to talk about?" Did I sound breathless? What was wrong with me?

"Um... So, I've been friends with Chyna for a while." He cupped my elbow and guided me around a protruding tree root in the sidewalk. "She talks about you all the time. I feel like I know you already."

I bit my lip as I noticed how soft his short hair looked, and those dimples in his cheeks weren't bad-looking either. He was on the tall-ish side. I loved tall men. "Yeah?"

"I was wondering…this is going to sound ridiculous." He stopped walking and grabbed my hand, pulling me to a stop. He stepped closer and leaned down. "Promise me you won't say no."

My heart lodged in my throat. I hadn't been asked out in so long. I couldn't even remember the last time it'd happened. It had never happened with someone as cute as Taylor. Oh, boy, this was going to be it. My new page. "I-I won't say no."

"I want you to put in a good word for me with Chyna. I want to ask her out, but I'm afraid she may have friend zoned me. I thought that if you mentioned to her that we met and that you thought I'd be good for her…"

My shoulders fell and I stepped away from him. Of course. Chyna. What had I been thinking? Men weren't interested in women like me. Especially not after they met my similar looking but infinitely more attractive twin. Plain, boring women like me didn't stand a chance when the Chyna's of the world were single and available.

I was suddenly furious, but mostly at myself. How could I think that a man as cute as Taylor would actually want to ask *me* out?

"Is that weird? I mean, I know it's weird, but I really like her."

I pulled my hand away and shoved it into my purse, feeling around for my keys somewhere in the bottom of the damned bag. The sooner I could get away, the better. "Chyna dates whoever she wants to date, Taylor."

"But—"

"I'm sorry, but I have some Ramen noodles and hot cocoa waiting for me. Buh-bye!"

So much for turning a new page.

4

CEZAR

"Beast and Sky are sucking face constantly and it's so nasty —all tongue and slobber. It's disgusting to see my aunt making out with *anyone*." Casey faked a gag and fell back on my couch. "Besides, I like hanging out here. You have games."

"You really need the internet, though," Nick, Casey's older brother, said as he sank into the large couch beside Casey. "We could play against people other than you, Cezar. Sorry for the brutal honesty, but you suck balls."

I let out a tiny puff of fire at them. Just enough to make them jump. "I don't suck. I blow. Fire."

Casey cheered and sat up straighter. "That. Was. Awesome! Can you take us for a ride later?"

I grinned and shrugged. "Maybe."

The truth was, I liked the two younglings. They were pleasant company even if they were, at fourteen and sixteen, mere babes. I hadn't seen those ages in centuries—more than a handful of centuries. The young males were excitable and had a good energy. Beast's new mate, Sky was the owner of them. Not owner...guardian.

"What's wrong, Cezar?" Nick let his game controller hang limp in his hands as he stared over at me. "You don't seem like your usual carefree self today."

I ran my tongue over my teeth as I thought about my morning. I had spent several hours at a local park, lurking, hoping to run into my mate. For some reason, a tiny female had struck me repeatedly with her satchel, called me a pervert and told me to stop staring at the children. I didn't know what had upset her so much. I had no malintent towards the younglings. I simply longed to have some of my own. I ached to find my mate and start a family. Lately, with every day that passed, I found myself wondering more and more if that would ever happen. The whole morning had put a damper on my mood. How was I supposed to find a mate when I scared human females?

"Cezar?"

I shook my head and shrugged. "It's nothing."

"Come on. You can tell us. You can bro-share anything with us. We won't tell. Cross our hearts and hope to die." Casey smiled when he said it and I would have sworn I saw what the humans called *the devil* in his expression.

Sinking into the large chair across from them, I frowned. "It is mate stuff."

"Okay, I take back what I said about bro-sharing. Gross."

"Casey, shut up. You're too young for this kind of stuff,

anyway." Nick puffed out his chest. "I'm almost seventeen. I've had a couple girlfriends."

"You've had one girlfriend and she broke up with you because she caught you yanking it in her bathroom."

"Casey! This is why no one wants to tell you anything. 'Cross my heart and hope to die?' If that really worked, you'd have been dead and buried fifty times over by now."

I grinned. "In her *bathroom*?"

With beet red cheeks, Nick shrugged. "Well, she should've knocked. It wasn't completely my fault. Every time I went over there, her mom always walked around wearing these really short, low-cut dresses, and she kept bending over in front of me."

I nodded. "Two things. One. Stay away from that house. Females like that are bad news. Two. Just keep it in your pants until you're back home."

"Can we talk about anything else? Really? *Anything*?" He groaned and leaned back on the couch until he was practically lying down.

In an effort to save him, I cleared my throat. "I'm having trouble finding my mate."

Casey went into the kitchen and grabbed a bag of chips from the snack cupboard where I kept a stash of junk food for the boys when they came to hang out. On his way back, I caught an eye roll. "Why do you want one?"

Nick shook his head at his brother. "You just don't get it, Casey. Men *need* things."

I narrowed my eyes at him. "Men *need* things?"

Nick nodded, sitting back up. "Yeah. My dad told me about it. Men need to have chicks around for, you know, certain things. It's the same thing with mates, right?"

I rubbed the back of my neck. "No, Nick, females are not objects to be used to fulfill men's needs. Yes, as a part of my biology as a dragon male, I do need a mate to stay sane and level, but mates are also a responsibility—an honor. It is our responsibility as males to fulfill *their* needs, to make them happy. Having a mate should be like having a best friend—the very best friend."

I shook my head. "A male should never treat a female as though she exists solely to care for his needs. Mates should complete one another."

Casey was silent for a moment. Then, he met Nick's gaze and blew out a breath. "It's not like Mom and Dad, then, huh?"

Nick's expression turned somber. "Definitely not like Mom and Dad. That's not how it's supposed to be."

I moved across the room to sit in between them. Grabbing a controller, I grinned at them both and attempted to change the subject. "I've been practicing. I bet I can kick both your asses."

We played an intense game of Call of Duty: Black Ops 4 for the next twenty minutes until Casey paused it. "I got an idea, Cezar, why don't you look for a mate online?"

I flipped the controller back and forth in my hands. "Yes. That thought did occur to me but I haven't exactly figured that out yet."

"Dude. Go on the internet and get on one of those dating sites. You just sign up and start dating." Nick pulled a phone out of his pocket and tapped at the screen for a few seconds before passing it to me. "See? This is Tender."

"Why do you have this?"

He blushed sheepishly. "Uh, needs?"

"Does your aunt know about this?"

"Hellz naw! Are you crazy? She'd flip. She still treats me like I'm a thumb-sucking baby."

I sighed. He *was* a mere babe. I wasn't going to phrase it that way and hurt his feelings, though. "You do seem a little young to be searching out a mate."

"I'm not searching for a mate. I'm just searching for a date." He grinned. "Not that it's come in useful. At all. No one anywhere close to here uses this, apparently, unless they're over thirty and I'm not into old ladies."

I hit a button and pictures of females started popping up. In one of them I saw a cute, curly-furred puppy. I had never had a pet before but I had seen countless humans with them. It was adorable.

"Her?" Nick frowned. "Really?"

I looked up at him, confused. He was staring at the phone. "What?"

"*That's* the type of woman you're looking for?"

I considered the photo again, this time noticing the female. I shrugged. She was okay except I didn't feel any mate-pull towards her. "I was looking at her dog."

"Oh, man, this is going to be harder than I thought."

I shook my head and scanned through more photos. None of the females caught my eye and eventually I just handed the phone back to Nick. "I don't know."

"These are women suggested for me. You have to set up your own account and get your own matches." He tucked the phone away and grinned. "I could set up an account for you."

Even though he was the saner of the two young males, I was still leery of entrusting him with such a task. "I shall do that myself."

"How? You don't even have internet and your phone is about a hundred-years-old. You really need to step into the twenty first century, dude." Casey picked up my flip phone from the coffee table. "Does it even have Instagram?"

I ran my hands through my hair. The modern world was so confusing. I tried, but every time I learned something, eight more things popped up to remind me of my own ignorance. What the hell was an Instagram and how was I to obtain one?

"Seriously, Cezar, you're like someone's old grandpa who just can't keep up."

I growled at Casey and snapped my teeth threatening to eat him.

He was lucky I'd made a rule against eating humans.

5

CHERRY

Monday morning, the second week of carrying the title of librarian of the Brasseaux Public Library, Cameron looked at me with a questioning gaze. I couldn't help but send her back a narrow-eyed glare double dog daring her to say a word. I'd arrived late to work, and we'd been swamped since. I knew what she wanted to ask. She wanted to know what the heck had happened to me. I wish I knew myself. I'd been feeling, well, *off* for the past week. If I was superstitious and believed in hocus-pocus, I'd swear I was experiencing a premonition. That was hogwash, though.

At any rate, I hadn't been myself at all lately. I'd broken my glasses and had to secure them together with electrical tape. Then, being late to work? It was the first time I'd overslept in...ever. I'd barely had time to throw on my clothes before rushing out the door. I had a huge stain on one half of my white shirt because, in my haste, I'd spilled my coffee all down the front of it. To top it off, I'd fallen asleep the night before with wet hair and I now looked like I'd stuck my finger in a light socket. I was a hot mess and it wasn't even lunchtime yet.

Even if I did want to talk about it—which I didn't—I wouldn't know what to say. Especially not with Cameron, who looked especially well put-together today. And, not with my sister, who waltzed into the library looking like the dark bronze goddess she was.

"Cherry! Hey!" Chyna hurried over to the circulation desk and leaned over it to give me a hug. "I'm sorry I missed hanging out this weekend. I was working, stuck in this tiny little swamp that had a patch of quicksand...you don't even want to know. How was your weekend?"

I tucked my lips into my teeth and pointed at the tape holding the center of my glasses together. "I'm just trying to embody every nerd stereotype possible."

She winced sympathetically. "Not such a great weekend?"

"Nothing eventful. I stayed in and binge-watched Netflix. The highlight was when I knocked my glasses off while trying to paint my toenails and somehow managed to simultaneously smear polish on my sofa and crack my glasses in two while trying to find them."

"Sounds enthralling."

"Very. So, tell me more about this quicksand."

"Like I said, you don't want to know. I had to stop by and see you, though. Maybe we can do lunch?" She ran her hands over my hair and wagged her eyebrows at me. "I guess this isn't morning after hair, then?"

I slapped her hands away. "Quit teasing. Go back to whatever you were doing before you showed up to harass me."

"Well, actually, I'm also here on business. I need to do some research on this species of moss I found."

"And you call me enthralling."

"Yeah, yeah. I'll let you get back to what you were doing. I'll be working until lunch. Then, you can take me out." She looked down at my shirt and shook her head. "You're a hot mess, girl."

"I hate you."

She blew me a kiss. "Love you, too, sis." She wiggled her fingers at me as she walked off, leaving me to my work. Heads followed after her as she strolled towards the back of the library, to the back room that she loved to work in. Heads always turned when she walked by, but she rarely noticed. It was a private joke between the two of us that our mother gave us stripper names yet we were two of the least promiscuous women of any we knew. Looks-wise, Chyna could have raked in the dollars as a stripper. With her beauty, she probably could have retired already. She was as prudish as I was, though.

Self-consciously, I ran my hands over my hair trying to pat it down and blew out a quiet sigh. How my twin could spend all her time scouting around in the swamp and still look beautiful, I would never know. I couldn't make it from my house to the library without being a disheveled disaster.

Slipping into my small office, I closed the door and stepped into the attached bathroom. I had a quick second to asses my appearance and see if I couldn't do some damage control.

My naturally curly hair was practically standing on end in places. Frizzy and unruly, my hair was a product of my possibly Creole heritage. Although, since Chyna and I didn't really know our heritage, Creole was just a guess—albeit a good one given our thick, curly black hair and cocoa skin tone.

My shirt was a mess, too. Everything was a mess. With my taped-up glasses, I could've been in one of those eighties teen movies. Not as the underdressed, ditzy-but-hot girl, of course. Nope, no, I was one headgear away from being the posterchild for the classic nerd-girl breathing heavily in the background

Groaning, I dug through my purse looking for a headband or barrette. Something. But, nada. Well, I did find a mini hairbrush, but trying to tug it through my frizzy disaster was futile. I just scooped the whole thing up into a pony tail and secured it with a rubber band from my desk drawer. What I was left with was a poof ball at the back of my scalp that slightly resembled Peter's cottontail but, I supposed it was a mild improvement from the frizz halo I'd been sporting.

I went back out into the library and made my rounds, checking to see if any of the patrons needed anything. After helping find a book on monster trucks for a kid who couldn't seem to take his eyes off the tape on my glasses the entire time we interacted, I headed back towards the circulation desk. That was when the front doors opened and, almost as if in slow motion, a huge, hulking figure stepped through.

I stopped dead in my tracks. The air vent in front of the doorway caught his sun-streaked hair and gently blew it back. Sweet baby Jesus! He was like one of those billboard ads of a handsome leading actor in a Hollywood blockbuster. A rom-com. The man in the doorway was too big, too handsome, too fit, too everything to not be some sort of model or Hollywood movie star.

In response to the breeze from the air vent, he casually reached up and ran his fingers through his hair. Wow. Even his mannerisms were sexy. A leather jacket stretched tightly over thick arms and my entire body went limp. *To be that leather jacket hugging his body like that*, I thought with a desperate heat blooming south of my belly. Even from across the room, he was amazing to look at. I wasn't the only one who noticed, either. It was as though a hush had fallen over the library. Every head turned to look at him. Dead silence. It was so quiet you could have heard a pin drop. Slayer would've been so pleased.

I watched as he paused, furrowed his brow and tipped his head back slightly, almost as though he was sniffing the air. Then, his head swung quickly in my direction, as though he sensed me staring. With lightning reflexes, I flipped around and pressed myself flat against a bookcase, firmly out of his line of sight. What the hell was wrong with me? If the man needed help, I'd have to help him. That was my job. What was I hiding from? I was in charge.

Thinking about going out there and offering him help was paralyzing, though. He was too attractive and whatever was going on with my body—and something was definitely going on with my body—was terrifying. I couldn't do it, not even on a normal day, but the idea of trying to talk to him when my appearance was that of three day old roadkill? Nightmarish.

I looked down and found, standing at my feet, the same kid who had been staring at the tape on my glasses earlier. He was looking up at me in contemplation. Forcing a smile, one I was sure looked more like a grimace, I grabbed a book off the shelf and opened it. "Oh, here it is. Just the book I was looking for."

Peeking surreptitiously around the bookcase, I saw that the amazingly handsome man had settled in and was now seated in front of a computer at one of the media tables. He was still facing me. My feet were still heavy as lead. I couldn't move from my spot. I was just going to have to stay right where I was until he left. Hopefully, that would be soon.

6

CEZAR

Something was strange about the place. I'd sensed it as soon as I walked in, but I couldn't put my finger on it. I glared down at the computer in front of me and rolled my neck. As hard as I tried to fit in, technology was still a struggle. I was too big for the tiny little devices, too. My fingers were too large for the keyboard and I didn't understand all the options. Right then, I was trying to figure out why the machine didn't accept any of the passwords I gave it.

My already irritated dragon roared flames in my head. Something in the library had roused him. He'd normally have been peacefully sleeping the day away while I did whatever I had to do, but he was wide awake and practically pacing. There was a scent in the building that was agitating —arousing, might have been a better word. It was fresh and sweet. I couldn't place it, but my dragon seemed to recognize the scent. Maybe it was something from our old world. That was nearly impossible, though.

Even as I thought up different passwords and typed them in, my mind wandered, trying to place the incredible smell. I looked around the table and smiled at the humans sitting there. They were staring at me like I'd grown out my tail, especially a youngling with face full of freckles.

"Computers, huh?" I shrugged and looked back down at my own work space. The computer dinged, telling me it didn't like the password I'd chosen. Again. My annoyance multiplied. I rubbed my hands over my face and blew out a slow breath. It didn't like any of my choices. What did the flaming thing want from me? How was I supposed to know what to type in?

The hair rose at the back of my neck and I adjusted myself in the chair that was too small. I felt as though I was being watched. I looked up again and found that I was. I was still being stared at intensely by the people around me. But, that's not what felt so off. It was something else. My gaze searched farther out into the room and caught a little glimpse of movement behind a book case. A fluffy, black poof of hair. I could still see it, sticking out slightly. A female?

"Do you need some help, sir?"

The female standing next to me was smiling. As she looked from my computer screen to my face, she raised her brows quizzically. My dragon withdrew and tried to back away from her. She was all wrong. She smelled wrong. There was something in here that was delectable, but this female was not it. Fortunately, I'd always had good control over my dragon. "I, uh, can't figure out a password."

"It's right here, silly." She pointed to a little piece of paper taped to the desk. "Every computer has a different password.

It's just the way the system is set up for some reason. It's just Library, pound, number 6. Capital L."

I read the paper and slumped in my chair feeling like a fire-mouthed idiot. I tried typing in the password. Another negative. I groaned. "It is not working."

She leaned in closer. "Let me."

Her small fingers typed faster than I had ever seen anyone type and then the computer made a happy sound and another screen came up. A picture of a long, narrow road with colorful trees on both sides. It was a rendition of the current season in the new world. Autumn. I leaned closer to study it. It was quite lovely. There had been no seasons in the old world. It had always been hot, unless it was freezing. Nothing in between like the new world's autumn.

"Do you need anything else?"

I shook my head, eager to be rid of her. It was humbling displaying one's inadequacies for all to see. I just wanted to figure out the dating site and then maybe sniff around the place to find out where that delectable scent was coming from.

"Just let me know if you change your mind."

I grabbed the controller thing and watched as the arrow on the screen moved around. I had to figure out how to get to the internet. Maybe if I just typed in the name of the site? I punched the keyboard, one button at a time, but nothing happened. Groaning, I looked around again. I didn't want to ask the female for additional help, but I also didn't know how to make the computer work.

Once again, I caught movement behind the shelf, a black poof that bobbed and swayed. It reminded me of the tail of the small creature called a bunny rabbit. I continued to stare until it disappeared fully behind a wall of books. I had an incredible urge to follow it, to go see what was going on. The strong urge itself was curious, but I'd come to the library for a reason. I had an important mission—one might say a life or death mission.

I hit buttons on the computer until something popped up, covering the picturesque autumn scene. There was a bar that said search and I tapped away at the computer, typing in the website Nick had told me about, hoping that I was doing it correctly. A few seconds passed and then a page full of text came up, some of it in different colors, all of it incoherent. I leaned back in my seat and sighed. It all looked like gibberish. Maybe I'd just go back to the park and take my chances. I shuddered remembering the shrill cries of the small female who tried to pummel me with her handbag.

I picked up the controller and tried to move it around the page. When the little arrow didn't move, I closed my eyes and took a deep breath. I could do this. I'd had trouble with my television at first, too. But, I'd read the user's manual twice and finally managed to get everything to work the right way. I could conquer the small controller, too. There was no user's manual for the controller, though. I moved it around, trying again to make it work. When nothing happened, I slapped the thing against my thigh hoping to wake it up.

The cracking sound drew surprised gasps, open-mouths and wide-eyes from around the table. Instead of just heads turning my way, entire bodies shifted to face me. I winced

Fire Breathing Cezar

and looked down at the controller in my hand. I'd crushed it. Accidentally, of course.

"I'm telling!" The freckle faced youngling pointed his little finger at me and wagged it in the air. My dragon strongly urged me to bite it off. Instead, I kept my reaction to a low, menacing snarl. The youngling's eyes rounded and he jumped up from his seat and ran off.

I scowled and reminded myself that in this world, it was not okay to hang younglings upside down and shake them to teach them manners.

Dropping the pieces of the controller on the table, I ran my now sweaty palms over my thighs. Between the delicious aroma in the room and the fucking baffling computer, my dragon was ready to break free and set the place aflame.

With interest, though, I noticed that the freckle faced youngling ran towards where I'd seen the black puffball. I listened intently hoping to hear something said, or better yet, hoping the owner of that ball of fluff would come into view.

7

CHERRY

If Jimmy Long didn't get the holy heck away from me, I was going to trip him the next time he walked by, I'd swear to Jesus. The little boy was always tattling on someone and there he was at it again. This time he was tattling on a grown man. The grown man who'd turned me into a quivering, cowardly mess. I was hiding. Still. Hiding like a scaredy cat. Not well enough, of course, that Jimmy hadn't found me.

I'd seen the man struggling. I hadn't expected him to shatter the mouse he was using, but he was awfully big. And strong. I fanned myself and pressed my back against the wall of the little nook I was in behind the bookshelf. And what was wrong with me? Why was my body overheating and why was I reacting like a frightened child?

"Well, Ms. Cherry, are you going to do anything?"

I snuck a quick glance around the corner and spotted the hottie looking in my direction. Jerking back around, I squeezed my eyes shut for a minute and shook my hands out.

Fire Breathing Cezar

"Ms. Cherry?"

"It's fine, Jimmy." I ground the words out harsher than I meant to and forced a smile to my face. "Sorry. I'm just looking for something right now. Why don't you go ask Cameron to help the man?"

"Cameron already tried to help him."

"Send her back over." I spoke through gritted teeth.

Jimmy pouted and went off in search of Cameron. I figured she wouldn't be far from the guy. Cameron loved men and was an expert at flirting with the opposite gender. There was no way that guy wasn't front and center on her radar right about then.

I backed farther into my hiding spot and rubbed the stress out of my forehead. My glasses fell off the tip of my nose and I caught them roughly as they fell. I felt the pieces twist in opposite directions and groaned as they loosened themselves even more from the tape I'd wrapped around them. The tape wasn't going to hold out for much longer.

It was silly that I was hiding, but there was something so overwhelmingly five-alarm about the way my body was reacting to the handsome man that I didn't think I could tolerate being any closer to him. He was beautiful, like a Roman statue or something, and I looked like a re-heated death casserole. I needed help. I was behaving crazy-like, but I couldn't seem to help it.

After a few seconds, Cameron appeared at my side. "One of the visitors needs you. *Demands* you, actually."

I flitted around with a book. "You can't handle it? I'm very busy right now. I'm working. On something."

"You're not working on anything. If I didn't know any better, I'd say you were hiding back here." She flicked the ponytail ball at the back of my head. "Not that I can blame you for hiding."

"Cameron." I blew out a breath and shook my head. "Just go help him."

As she walked away with an eye roll, I stayed where I was and prayed that she could help him and get him going on his way as soon as possible. Cameron was capable of showing him anything he needed to know about the computer. He didn't need me. Not at all.

I poked my head out enough to look over at them and inhaled sharply when I saw Chyna stop next to him and Cameron. She smiled at the man and I felt myself growing irrationally angry as she reached up to run a hand through her beautiful, well-conditioned hair. Her shirt drew up to show off a couple inches of her flat stomach and, even though I knew my sister well enough to know that she would never be intentionally flirty, I still grew irate for some reason.

When I looked back at the man, though, he wasn't noticing Chyna and her smooth, mocha skin or her flat belly or her perfect hair. In fact, he was barely noticing that Cameron or Chyna were in the room. He was staring directly at me. When our eyes met, I startled so hard that I involuntarily let out a weird little yelping-squealy-squawk and flung myself back into the nook behind the bookshelf. *Shit. That was really loud.*

A few seconds later, Cameron and Chyna were both standing in front of me, arms crossed over their chests.

Cameron pursed her lips and regarded me with a hard stare. "That man over there is insisting that you be the one to help him and you're back here hiding from him. What's going on?"

"Do you know him?" Chyna's brows were furrowed and she studied my reaction closely. I just shrugged and shook my head, afraid of what my voice might sound like if I tried to use it.

"Do you want me to toss him out on his ass?" Cameron's jaw locked and her hands flew to her hips. "Because I will."

Chyna scowled at Cameron and inched closer to me, closing Cameron out. "Wait a sec, this is just you running like a scared bunny from any man that might show an interest in you, isn't it?"

Well, if the hair fit... I ran my hands over my head again and fussed with my shirt. "Chyna..."

She flicked the end of my nose. "Sorry for this, sis."

Before I could even ask what she was sorry for, she grabbed me and with both hands, shoved me out from behind the bookshelf. I stumbled, let out another weird yelping squeak, and windmilled my arms to catch myself. When I did catch myself, every eye in the place was on me.

My cheeks burned bright red as I turned to give my sister a pissed-off glower. There was no way I could avoid the man after that stunt. His mouth was open slightly in surprise and he was staring a hole right through me. My head, of its own accord, turned in his direction. It was like I couldn't stop it. My eyes glanced up and then, from across the room, our gazes met, held, and locked. And, oh, talk about going weak at the knees.

My skin burned even hotter and I forgot for a second that I was a complete train wreck. My breath caught in my throat and I wondered if I'd even be able to move my legs enough to cross the room. My feet had melted into the hardwood floor.

"What are you doing?" Chyna's sharp whisper broke through my stupor. "Get over there!"

I closed my eyes and breathed a deep inhale. I didn't know what was wrong with me. It wasn't like he was the first attractive man I'd ever seen in my twenty-nine years. Although, as I made myself take a step towards him, and then another, I felt that I could honestly say he was the *most* attractive man I'd ever seen. Blonde hair a little too long, eyes a brilliant green, and a dangerous edge that made him seem so out of place in a quaint little branch library.

I forced myself to walk forward and stopped within a few feet of him. Trying to smile, I focused on a spot on the wall just over his left shoulder. I started to speak and my voice came out a crackle, so I had to clear my throat and try again. "H-how can I help you?"

My eyes flicked over his computer and I made a face before I could help myself. He was looking up a dating website. Why the hell was a man who looked like him on a dating website? I had a feeling he could walk down the sidewalk in a burlap sack and get propositioned every few feet.

"Hello." Of course, he had a deep, masculine voice that sent tingles through me. Of course. Low, velvety and smooth, it was like a verbal caress.

I met his gaze and swayed just the slightest bit. Warmth coursed down my spine and pooled in my lower belly. I took a step back, feeling totally unhinged by all the sensations I was feeling. "Hi."

He stood up and closed the distance between us. His eyes traveled over my body and face, pausing at my hair. The corner of his mouth twitched. Great. He was amused by my hair.

I sucked in a sharp breath and took another step back. He was putting out predatory vibes to the extreme and I suddenly felt like a gazelle being stalked by a lion. It was scary. What was even scarier was how much I liked it.

"Well, Miss Cherry, are you going to yell at him for breaking the mouse, or what?"

I was finally grateful for Jimmy's big mouth. I spun to face him and nodded. "Yeah. Yeah, I should do that."

The gorgeous man's face fell. "You should yell at me?" His voice dipped even lower and his eyes darkened slightly. His tongue snaked out as he licked his full lower lip.

"Yeah, mister, you can't go around breaking stuff in the library, right Miss Cherry? Tell him."

"I...um..." I licked my own dry lips and watched as his eyes followed my tongue. I thought I heard a low growling sound emanate from his chest. But, that was crazy. It was at that point that my supply of courage was depleted. "Actually, I have something to do. Bye!"

And, I ran.

8

CEZAR

I found her!

Petite, curvy, brown skinned, and beautiful but very timid, she backed away from me and then flat out turned and ran. Strange. But, if she thought running from me would stop me, she was in for a surprise. I left the computer behind without a second thought. Fortunately, the dating site was a thing of the past. I no longer needed it. I had found my mate. She was everything I could want and more.

I trailed behind her, my longer, stronger legs eating up twice the distance of her shorter ones. "I am Cezar."

She jumped, not realizing I was right behind her, and then glanced back at me. "Um...yeah."

I stepped around two small human younglings and watched as my mate, Miss Cherry, grabbed a stack of books. I gently took them from her. No need for her to carry anything when I'm around. And, hopefully, I would never be far from her side. "Please, allow me."

Fire Breathing Cezar

She looked confused. "I can do it..."

"Please allow me to help." I smiled at her and shrugged. "It is an honor to assist a beautiful woman such as yourself."

She stopped moving and I nearly bumped into her. "What are you doing?"

"Carrying your books?"

She shook her head and wagged her finger at me. "No. This. Carrying my books? Calling me beautiful? I've got a mirror and I've looked into it today. I'm under no delusions about my appearance. Are you trying to make up for breaking my mouse?"

"I did not break a mouse." It was the second time I was hearing about a broken mouse and I was getting confused. "I am an excellent predator. I would have known if a mouse had been nearby."

She frowned. "The computer mouse. The thing you shattered?"

"The controller?"

"What?" She started walking again and led us into a hallway of books.

"What?" I followed her.

"What?" she repeated. "Yeah, the mouse. I guess you could call it a controller. Anyway, you broke it. What gives?"

"I did not do it purposely. I believe it was broken before I crushed it. It would not work."

She took a book from me and slid it onto the shelf. "It wasn't broken."

"Then why would it not work?"

"Maybe because you were holding it in the air like it was some kind of toy airplane."

"Please, allow me to take you on a date tonight. Or, now?"

"What?" Cherry looked up at me, her face turning a bright red. It looked beguiling on her.

"What?" That was what human men did, was it not? They took their females places and called the outing a date. I didn't want to be too pushy, but I was eager to change the topic from the broken controller and talk about the two of us. Perhaps I'd phrased it wrong. "May I take you to dinner? On a date? Or, if you prefer, we could go for coffee, or to a movie, or to a musical event."

She backed up against the shelving unit behind her and bit her lower lip. "*What*?"

What a firemouthed fool I was! I placed the books on the floor and stepped closer to her. Of course! It was obvious now. My mate was hard of hearing. I raised my voice. "May I take you on a date?"

"Why are you yelling?" she hissed, staring up at me with confusion and a touch of anger in her expression. I'd gotten close enough to her that when she turned and moved away from me, her puff ball hit me in the chest. It not only looked interesting, it smelled amazing. She smelled clean and fresh like dew on newly sprouted grass.

"I assumed you were hard of hearing. You keep asking, 'what'." From that close, I could see that her brown eyes had bursts of gold in the center of them. Mesmerizing. Her skin was the silkiest thing I'd ever seen. It was the color of a sweet coffee beverage. I wanted to run my fingertips over it and feel her, all of her—or better yet, my lips. Her curves were mouthwatering, and I imagined they would be even more enticing without all the loose, bulky clothing.

I ran my hands through my hair, to keep from grabbing her. That was a no-no in the human mating rituals, but instinctual for dragons. I had finally found my mate. I was so eager and ready to begin a life with her, to learn everything about her and experience everything together. "I am asking you to go on an outing with me. I will take you wherever you wish to go."

"Stop it." She turned and grabbed the books off the ground, presenting me with a beautiful view of her full, round bottom, and then hurried away again. "I don't know what your game is, buddy, but I'm not amused."

I followed her, as I would always from that day forth. "I have no game. I would like to date you."

"No."

I froze, that one lone word paralyzing me. I felt as though my heart dropped to my toes, crumbling to pieces at my feet. "W-why?"

"Because. Because, that's why."

Was it because I'd been looking at a dating site? Perhaps that was the reason for her rejection. Perhaps if I explained..."I was simply trying to find my mate. I mean, a date. I was trying to find a *date*. Then, when I saw you, I knew you were the female I was looking for. You are perfect. Everything a dra—*male* could want. Please allow me to court you. That is what males and females do, is it not?"

She turned a corner and we were in another hall of bookshelves. It was darker there and she stretched up to put another book away. I caught my breath as her shirt came up the slightest bit to reveal a bare strip of smooth skin at her waist.

"You are too much. Leave me alone."

"Leave you...*alone*?" Was she serious? She did not accept me? Did she not feel the magic between us? My chest ached and my dragon roared his displeasure. "You are joking, right?"

"No, I'm not joking. I don't know what you're trying to pull, but this isn't funny. I am dead serious. Leave. Me. Alone."

I did not want to upset her any more than I already had, so I backed away slowly. "I apologize for whatever I did that upset you. I promise I will learn to please you. I have nothing but the best of intentions."

She furrowed her brows and shook her head. "Just go."

Forcing my body to move away from her was torture. I felt as though I had cinderblocks for feet as I dragged them from where my mate stood. Everything in me, male and dragon, longed to stay and be near her. I knew from research that modern human women did not appreciate when males just took what they desired. Human females wanted to be listened to and heard. I would treat my mate the way she wished to be treated. I turned and walked out, feeling like the world was caving in on me.

I stopped just outside the library doors and tried to calm my dragon. I would fix this. Things would be okay. At least I'd found her—I knew she existed and who and where she was.

I just had to figure out how to win her over. She was definitely mine. I knew that without a doubt. As soon as I'd seen her, I'd known. I simply had to convince her of that fact. I foolishly believed she would feel the same pull towards me but I was mistaken. I would, perhaps need to consult with Beast's mate, Sky, about how such things worked for human females.

I might need to revisit my research as well. I thought I knew how modern human men wooed their females, but I had not done well. I had a stack of books back at the castle on the subject and I had studied as much as I could find about it. I would re-examine them and do all that they said. I would do anything to prove to her that she belonged to me.

Mating in this world wasn't as easy as it had been back in our old world. Evidently, we had to work much harder. I thought of my beautiful, curvy, brown mate with the fluffy hair. She was worth it. Beast had worked hard for his Sky and he was happier than any dragon. Ever.

I would do the same.

9

CHERRY

The next several days passed in a blur of overwhelming lunacy. It seemed that each hour that passed brought more gifts. I was starting to think that the man was one brick short of a full load. Cezar. What kind of name was that, anyway? Cajun? Creole? Everything about him was unusual. The way he'd followed me around the library, asking me on a date. The way he'd provoked such a physical response from me. Plus, I'd chastised the man. That was so out of character for me, but it was because I was freaked out by the way my body responded to him. All of it was crazy, but the craziest was the fact that he really seemed to think I would believe that a man who looked like him, Mr. Hollywood, would want to go out with a woman who looked like me, Nerd Girl.

Each new gift that arrived made me think that I was stuck in a surreal dream. First, it'd been flowers. Huge bouquets. The first practically engulfed the entire circulation desk. Then, two more came. I'd had to divide them into smaller bouquets and scatter them on different tables around the library. I couldn't say I hated having their beauty and the delightful scent around, though.

After the flowers, there had been the giant stuffed animals. I appreciated those, too. They decorated the children's corner nicely. Then, there were the treats. Boxes, baskets and bouquets of food covered the tops of the open surfaces—assorted chocolates, chocolate covered strawberries, chocolate truffles, fruit and nut baskets, fruit bouquets. The fruit and nuts fed Cameron, Marilyn and me during our shifts. Chyna also took a whole tray of chocolate covered strawberries. Every woman who saw them seemed to be beside herself, talking about how lucky I was and encouraging me to snatch Cezar up while I could.

I wouldn't admit it to anyone, but it did make me feel pretty special and I was rather flattered by all the attention. Never before in my life had anyone done anything like that for me. But, then, there was that niggling at the edge of my brain telling me it was way weird and stalkerish for a virtual stranger to spend hundreds of dollars plying me with gifts. Especially a hot looking stranger.

The whole situation was getting a bit ridiculous. I had vowed to step outside my comfort zone a little where men and relationships were concerned, to turn a new page, but this shit was next level. It was a circus. A circus complete with a giant cake and a male singer dressed as a clown. Yep, more gifts. The last one had been the most unwelcome of all. I wasn't a fan of clowns, or singing telegrams. And, to top it off, he threw glitter at me. Glitter! In the library. Did he know how hard glitter was to get rid of? There was a reason it was deemed the herpes of the craft world.

When a box came with a diamond bracelet, it was the last straw. The one that broke the camel's back. I tried to refuse delivery, but that only resulted in an argument with a huffy postal delivery service woman. So, I gave it to Chyna. There was no way I was keeping diamonds.

By the end of the week I, and everyone around me, was sick to death of chocolate and the flowers were beginning to wilt. I was embarrassed and tired of trying to find spaces for the gifts. I was also starting to worry that Cezar might be dangerous. Although, he hadn't shown up again to the library, he'd only just spent a small fortune in gifts. I would have liked to say that I couldn't even remember the man's face, but that would have been a lie. His handsome visage was scalded into my memory banks. Every time I shut my eyes, I saw those blazing green eyes staring back at me, along with all the hurt and disappointment they'd displayed when I'd turned him down flat, pushed him away and told him to "just go".

He probably hadn't deserved that, but on the other hand, I was a little on edge at that point and wondering if I should consider filing charges against the man for stalking. Yet, it made no sense that a man as fine as him would be stalking *me*. People had started showing up in the library just to see what would be delivered next. It was chaos.

Friday night book club started no differently than the previous one. Marilyn got ready to read the latest passage from the book we were sharing that week while I got wine ready for everyone. Instead of the small group of women we usually had, the group had more than quadrupled in size. Interestingly, Slayer and her small posse were still there, too.

I could handle that. What I couldn't handle was Cezar striding in all sexy and hot with a huge grin on his face and a delicious smelling takeout bag in his hand. I hadn't seen him since that first day, and it somehow seemed that he'd gotten even handsomer over only a handful of days. In low slung jeans and a simple white T-shirt that stretched tightly over his chest and biceps, he had the swagger of James Dean. Only Cezar was much bigger. And better looking. His honey blonde hair was pulled back in a ponytail, and just long enough to fit into one. His eyes seemed to glow a bright green as they searched me out and stopped when they found me.

I was stunned stupid. As he came towards me, I wanted to run, but once again, I couldn't make my legs cooperate.

"Hello, Cherry." He stopped right in front of me and smiled. "You look beautiful this evening. Your hair is especially lovely."

I reached up and touched it self-consciously. It was normal, pinned back out of my face. "What are you doing here?"

"I wanted to bring dinner to share with you. And wine."

Marilyn appeared from behind me. "So, you're the stud muffin who keeps sending these unbelievable gifts."

He kept his eyes on me and nodded. "I am attempting to display my affection for Cherry and hoping my gifts will convince her to allow me to court her."

I made a face. Who talked like that? "Look, this has to stop. These gifts are too much."

"Nonsense, Cherry." Marilyn took the bottle of wine from him. "He saved the day. We needed another bottle."

"You are displeased with the gifts?" He looked genuinely confused—and hurt. Damn. "I thought females appreciated gifts to show affection."

"No. None of this is okay."

"Why not?"

"Because it's loco. You sent me diamonds. You don't even know me."

"I know enough to know you deserve diamonds."

"What could you possibly know about me that justifies diamonds?"

"That you are my...uh...that I like you. Very much. Why is that not enough?"

"What are trying to do? I don't trust this. You don't want a date with me. You want something else. I just don't know what."

He stepped closer to me. "You. I only want you."

I wanted to argue more, but Marilyn came up and grabbed him by his enormous bicep leading him away. "Come on, big fella. Even though this is technically a woman's book club, you brought wine so you're an honored guest tonight. Sit right here by our lovely head librarian." She waved to a folding chair that had magically appeared next to the one I had been sitting in before he showed up. "Sit. I'm about to start reading."

Oh, heaven help me! "No—"

"I would love to. Thank you." He smiled the biggest, broadest smile I'd ever seen, and nodded to the chair next to him, which, of course, I awkwardly plopped myself into. Leaning close to me, he whispered. "I do not understand why you think I would not want you, but I do. If you will only agree to a date, you will make me a very happy male, Cherry."

Marilyn cleared her throat and began reading.

> *"As Darius slammed Bethany against the bedroom wall, her legs straddled him and his molten member begged entrance to her slick love canal."*

My cheeks flamed. If ever the Earth could open a sinkhole and swallow me up, it would have been a stellar moment for it. As Marilyn was reading explicit erotica in front of the stranger who claimed to want to take me on a date, and who I thought was the sexiest man alive, I squirmed and wiggled in my folding chair. The other women in the group kept tossing heated looks over their shoulders at Cezar. Hussies. He noticed it, too, because he leaned closer to me to whisper in my ear.

"Why are they all looking at me like that?"

I shuddered in response to the deep timbre of his whisper, but also at the looks being thrown his way. What the hell? It was like feeding time in the lion's den and Cezar was the fresh meat. I almost felt worried that it would be the end of something that hadn't even started yet, and I found I didn't like the idea. The women looked so ravenous, but the man was *mine*. I glared at them, every single one, feeling uncharacteristically possessive of him. The man was *mine*. Wait, what? I didn't mean he was *mine* mine... Did I?

They should've been listening to Marilyn, anyway, who was doing a great job narrating an orgasm complete with alarmingly realistic moaning and grunting. I sat back in my seat and dug my balled up fists into my thighs.

Cezar shifted in his chair and leaned closer to me. "You have quite an interesting pastime."

I turned to tell him to stop whispering to me because it was doing things to my insides—and my outsides—and found his face a mere inch from mine. His breath brushed over my lips and the smell of fresh mint teased me. He was so handsome *and* he had fresh breath. And, lord help me, he was staring at me the way the other women in the room were staring at him. Like he was ready to gobble me up.

> *"...crying out in pleasure-fueled ecstasy that left her quivering as he continued to thrust inside of her until at last his passion juice filled her in warm bursts."*

I blinked and leaned away. What the actual hell was happening?

Cezar just sat back in his chair and cleared his throat. He tossed another look my way, but I quickly turned my head to face Marilyn. After she finished reading, it was time to discuss the book, but I didn't think I could manage it. I was feeling like a lit stick of dynamite that at any second was going to explode.

10

CEZAR

I had been doing what the books advised regarding human courting rituals. I sent every gift suggested, until finally, I decided it was time to go to her myself. I tried to be clever and bring the dinner date to her. She had to eat. Besides, I could not bear to be away from her for another day. So, I'd brought food and ended up joining a group of females as one of them read a story to us about humans fucking. Many of the females stared at me as though *I* was dinner. It had felt a bit awkward and uncomfortable until I'd smelled the sweet, enticing aroma of Cherry's arousal when I leaned in to whisper to her. Her scent was heavenly and it said to me that, despite her words, she desired me.

I knew then that I just needed to continue to have patience. What the books advised was working. After the human female finished reading, Cherry stood quickly and rushed from the group. I followed. My dragon was fighting for dominance. I had an innate instinct to overpower her and take her, mark her with my seed and fangs, claim her so all would know she was mine. Yet, I battled the desire. She was not a dragoness and I knew I must proceed that way humans conducted mating rituals—for my mate's sake. But first, I needed just a taste of her. Just a taste.

She disappeared into another one of the aisles of bookshelves and I followed behind her. She spun and opened her mouth, appearing as though she was about to speak in anger, but I had inhaled the scent of her arousal and I would not be deterred. I closed the gap between us, grabbing her, pulling her against me while I leaned down and captured her sweet lips with mine. This time, just this time, I fed my desire. She stumbled backwards and I followed, walking us steadily back until we reached the solid wall. Holding her against the wall, pressing my body against hers, I deepened the kiss. Head tilted, I slid my tongue across her lips as I ran my hands down her waist to grasp her ample hips. Her mouth tasted sweet as honey as my tongue swept in—a taste that exploded behind my eyes. My brain struggled to process the situation above the immense pleasure I felt.

The timid little librarian who acted as though she wanted nothing to do with me, threaded her fingers into my hair and gripped my head as though she was afraid I'd slip away. Her nails bit into my scalp and her tongue tangled with mine. She was a hot-blooded vixen. She wrapped one of her legs around mine using it to pull me closer as she rubbed against my hard length. Her soft curves were molded to me from her shoulder to her knees and I had never known a feeling of such excitement or bliss. When I cupped her plump bottom in my hands and raised her to stroke her core over my erect cock, her teeth bit down on my lip and she moaned into my mouth.

My dragon roared to the surface. My body threatened to grow larger with the transformation. Scorching heat pulsated from me as the need to claim my mate overwhelmed me. It was bloodlust, a lust like no other, urging me to sink my teeth into her soft flesh. I wanted to. I needed to.

"Cezar...Cezar, stop." Cherry's husky plea tore me from my haze. When I pulled back, she blinked up at me a few times and then shook her head. "There are people here. Patrons..."

It took a moment to process what she was saying, but then, I gently put her down and backed away. "Yes. You are right."

She stumbled slightly, but put her hand out to stop me when I tried to steady her. "I need to clean up here. I have...I need to work."

I watched her ass sway inside the baggy pants she wore. Those big, loose clothes did not fool me. I knew she had a stunning body underneath. I was glad she was hiding it from other males, though. She was mine.

That thought triggered something in my brain and I felt a bit ashamed. Yes, she was mine, and I had almost lost control. I needed to take better care of her. Humans didn't work the same way as dragons. I couldn't just tell her she was mine and watch her fall to her knees and beg me to mate her as dragon females of the old world would have done.

Human females were much more confusing, but my mate was worth it and I would do whatever it took to make her accept me as hers. I would find a way, and I would persevere. When she turned the corner and I lost sight of her, I followed. The need to keep her near me was overwhelming. I trailed behind, unable to take my eyes from the timid little female who'd just proven to me she held a scorching passion below her surface. I wanted her more than any treasure that had ever existed. She was my treasure to be horded and guarded, worth more than gold or the finest jewels.

I waited for her as the other women left, one by one until I found myself alone in the library with Cherry again. She was in her office working at her computer, but it was not long before she returned.

"Oh." She seemed surprised when she spotted me leaning against the door. "You're still here."

"I would not leave you alone. It is dark out. I will walk you home." I saw her start to form a protest and I cleared my throat. "Please. Allow me. Please."

She hesitated for a moment and then shrugged. "Okay, fine. It's not far, though."

I held the door open and then followed her through. "Tonight was...interesting."

"This whole week has been interesting, thanks to you. You've turned my world upside down. When I think that just one week ago, I walked home with a guy who..."

I bit back a growl. "There is another male?! Another male is also vying for your attentions?"

She snorted. "No. You didn't let me finish. He walked me home so he could convince me to set him up with my sister. Chyna. You met her."

I shook my head. "I do not think so."

"You did. She's my twin. Looks just like me only thinner and prettier. She stopped to help you the day you broke the mouse."

"I told you, I broke no mouse. There was no mouse." I sighed. "I do remember there being other people there that day, but I could not remember anything about them. Not with you there."

Cherry stopped walking and stood with her arms crossed over her chest. "What do you want from me?"

Was it a trick question? What did she mean what did I want? I rubbed my forehead. "Right this moment? Or do you mean later?"

"Why are you saying all these incredible things and sending me all these amazing gifts? Why did you show up with food tonight...food that we left behind in the library, by the way."

"Because I wish to take you on a date. Am I not explaining myself correctly?"

"And, why do you phrase things so oddly at times? And how do you not know what a mouse is?"

I ran my hands through my hair, frustrated by the barrage of questions. "I do know what a mouse is. A small rodent. Bottom of the food chain."

"Oh, sweet baby Jesus!" She started walking again, faster. "This is all too weird. Men who look like you do not go for women like me. Women like my sister, maybe, but not me. Not to mention the fact that you met me on a day when my hair looked like I'd gone through the automated carwash and my glasses were held together with electrical tape. I don't believe any of this. And, by the way, I'm not into kink, I don't go clubbing and my idea of a great evening is staying home, curling up on the sofa and watching TV or reading a good book."

I gently took her arm and pulled her to a stop again. "While I like your hair the way it is this evening very much, it looked lovely before."

"Now I know you're full of shit!"

I did not know what I had said that time to anger her, but her temper seemed to be emerging once again. "Why do you say that?"

"*Why do you say that?*" She mimicked me in a whiney tone that set my teeth on edge.

"I do not sound like that."

"*I do not sound like that.*" She walked a few feet more and turned to go up the steps of a very small house sandwiched between two other very small houses. "Thank you for walking with me. Now, go home. We're done here."

I stomped up the stairs after her, my own anger getting the best of me. "You mock me and now you are going to run from me and close the door in my face?"

"Um, that's the idea, yeah."

"Is there a reason you treat me so poorly? Is there a reason you do not like me?"

She started to mock me again but I grabbed her face and kissed her, effectively shutting her up. I backed her against her door and kissed her until we both had to break apart, gasping for air.

"T-That. You make me feel like...that...too much." She licked her lips and stared up at me with her chest rising and falling in a quick rhythm. "I gotta go."

I slowly nodded and backed away. Her body was saying something completely different than her mouth, but the books all stated that I must listen to what her mouth said. Even if I did not want to, and even if she did not mean it. "Goodnight, then."

Cherry slipped into her house and I heard her panting on the other side of the door, but I forced myself to descend the stairs. There would be another chance. I would never give up. It would not come soon enough to comfort me—or my dragon, but it would come.

I was turning to leave when I heard the sound of the door sliding open again. I jerked back around. Time seemed to stand still. Cherry was at the top of the stairs with her shoulders tensed, fists balled up at her sides and her lip caught between her teeth.

By the look in her eyes, I knew she had changed her mind.

11

CHERRY

Foolish or not, I didn't want to let Cezar leave. The real reason I was treating him so badly was that I was drawn to him like a moth to a flame; everyone knew that only ends in immolation.

I wanted him. But I didn't want to want him. I'd never in my life been touched or kissed the way he touched and kissed me and my body responded by heating to the intensity of an inferno. I was completely out of control when he was near and I hated that. But, I loved it, too.

I stood at the top of my stairs, looking down at him, well, *over* at him since he was so tall we were almost at eye level. A part of me wanted to keep the door closed and lock him safely out of my life. The keyword there was *safely*. It was so tempting to remain safely cocooned in the modest life I'd built. Cezar threatened that. The other part of me was drawn to his passion, his danger, his fire.

I had promised myself to turn a new page, specifically where the issue of my virginity was concerned, and as though the universe heard me loud and clear, there was my chance, standing across form me staring at me under the moonlit sky with eyes full of a ferocious hunger. A hot, hunky, sexy, irresistible chance.

If he hadn't changed his mind, that was. I opened my mouth to ask him if he still wanted me, but Cezar took the few stairs in one giant step and was in front of me in a split second grasping my face in his hands, dropping his head to mine, teasing me with his soft, velvety lips while his tongue invaded my mouth bold and demanding.

My back hit the door. Slipping his hands down to my ass, he easily lifted me into his arms and held the bottom of my thighs. We clung together like perfectly snug-fitting puzzle pieces. He walked us into my house and didn't even pull away from my mouth to shut the door.

"Bedroom." His voice was rough and husky.

The angel on my shoulder was whispering that maybe I should slow things down. I didn't know anything about Cezar. He was a complete stranger and possibly an obsessive stalker and, if so, I might be fanning flames. Instead, the devil on my other shoulder was rooting on behalf of my sex-starved body which was aching for the man whose passion enveloped me and turned me on like I've never been turned on before. "To the right."

With my thighs locked around his waist, he turned right and carried me to my bedroom without removing his mouth from mine. Only when we bumped into the table in my hallway did he break away and pepper kisses down my neck. "You taste so delicious."

I buried my hands in his hair and held on through the torturous pleasure. My whole body felt like lava flowed through my veins. The spots on my neck where his lips had been still burned sending waves of heat up and down my spine. A tornado of sensations whirled through me. I was finally going to know what the whole sex thing was about and I wanted to. I wanted it so badly.

Cezar raked his teeth over my collar bone and growled. "Remove your clothing."

In response to his demand, I dropped my legs and slid down his body. Once my feet were on solid ground, I tugged the bottom of my shirt and yanked it over my head. I shoved my pants down and stood in front of him in just my bra and panties. It wasn't so much confidence that filled me as it was the desperate need to feel more of his touch on more of my skin.

He moaned low in his throat and ripped his own shirt over his head. So much tanned muscle came into view that I felt my mouth water. A swath of blonde chest hair decorated his chest and then in a thin line, led down to disappear into his pants.

"Take off your breast covering."

"Take off your pants."

One side of his mouth quirked up in a crooked grin. "You're much more than an innocent little librarian, aren't you, my Cherry?"

I'd been unhooking my bra, but I froze when he said that. Casually, like it was no big deal, I let the bra drop and freed my breasts.

"Actually...I'm a virgin. It's not a big deal, though. I don't want it to be a big deal, okay?"

He toed off his boots and pushed his pants down and kicked them off before standing back up and wrapping his arms around my waist. "I know you are. And it is a big deal. I will be careful with you."

I shook my head. "I don't need careful."

Cezar took my hand and placed it over his erection. "You will need careful."

My eyes went wide at his enormous size. "Oh, I don't know if that there's gonna fit in this here. Um, well, careful is good, then."

He caught the band of my panties with his thumbs and pulled them down, dropping to his knees in front of me. I sucked in a sharp breath and reached for anything to keep me stable on my feet. I ended up with my hands locked in his hair which had, by then, been pulled free from the ponytail it had been in at the start of the evening.

"You smell so incredible. I cannot resist your tempting aroma any longer." To make his point, he buried his face between my legs and inhaled.

I gasped and tried to move away, but he gripped my hips hard and held me steady. "Cezar..."

He raised his head and met my gaze. His was hot and intense. "I need to taste you, my Cherry."

"I never—"

He buried his face again and hooked one of my legs over his shoulder to spread me wider. I balanced precariously and then nearly melted when I felt the first flick of his tongue across my most sensitive area. The way he delved in, the wild sensation of his hot mouth on me, threatened to knock me over.

His tongue slipped lower and dipped between my folds, swirling as it went. Then, he treated me to long swipes, up and down that threatened to buckle my knees. His dusting of stubble was rough against my thighs and lower lips, and it added to the wild feelings he was awakening in me. With my hands locked in his hair, I found myself pulling his mouth harder into me. I was unrestrained. When his tongue plunged even deeper, I arched my back and yanked harder at his hair. It was as though his tongue was everywhere all at once, tantalizing every sensitive nerve ending.

"Cezar..." I moaned his name and swayed as I felt a buildup occurring. Tension, strung tighter and tighter, building until it was almost painful. All my muscles contracting, my heart pounding, I felt like I'd die before I reached the pinnacle.

Then, mercifully, Cezar's mouth closed over my clit and he sucked. His teeth scraped sides of the oversensitive bud and I came with a loud, uninhibited scream. The pounding heat in my veins replaced the tension and flowed to my pulsing, quivering core. My toes curled into the rug under my feet and I gasped for breath as wave after wave of pleasure rolled through me. Yet, it wasn't enough. Even through the most powerful orgasm I'd ever experienced, I wasn't satiated. The pulsing became searching...for something, someone. No, not someone, Cezar.

"Cezar, more. Please."

He picked me up and tossed me onto the bed like I weighed nothing. I bounced and landed on top of my throw pillows. They propped me up enough that I could easily watch as Cezar pushed his briefs down and then stood before me, naked and glorious. Tall, tan, muscled, and surprisingly sun kissed, his erect cock stood out proudly in front of him. He was beautiful.

"You taste like the sweetest nectar when you climax." He pulled one knee up on the bed and took his much larger than average member in his hand. "Everything about you makes me hard, Cherry."

Still trembling, I pulled myself to my knees and reached my shaky hands out to take a hold of him. As I touched his sex, I felt a pulse of desire so strong that it took my breath away. Thick and heavy, he was surprisingly hard, like steel, yet silky smooth. The veins that stood out sent shivers down my spine as my fingers trailed over them. I wasn't even embarrassed that it was the first time that I'd ever touched a man that way. "Can I?"

He groaned and shook his head. "I can't control myself right now, Cherry."

Feeling reckless, I shrugged. "Don't, then."

12

CEZAR

My sweet little mate looked anything but innocent as she gazed up at me with her big brown eyes only slightly hidden behind her dark-rimmed glasses. Her dark, curly hair was falling down around her shoulders and breasts. She looked like a siren. A siren who would forevermore lure me to her with her call.

I was struggling to keep my beast in check. I had to remember that Cherry was a human and a virgin. I would need to be gentle with her, and proceed slowly. It would not be easy. I wanted nothing more than to bury my cock into her and feel her pulsate around me as I sank my teeth into her neck and tasted her sweet life force.

Cherry had other ideas, though. She crouched forward on her elbows and looked up at me, her ass completely in the air, unknowingly torturing me while I struggled to maintain control. "Tell me if this is no good."

I raised an eyebrow and was about to ask what she was referring to when she ran her tongue over the head of my cock. All my blood instantly surged to that very spot to meet her tongue. My hands were balled tightly into fists at my side. I had to blink a few times to make sure I was still standing there on the Earth. "W-what are you doing, little mate?"

She took my cock past her lips and the soft walls of her mouth encased me like warm velvet, sliding over me inch by inch. Then, she retracted her mouth with a suctioning, and I almost followed her with my hips. "I mean, I've never done it before and I don't really know how, but I'm attempting to give you a blow job. Is it terrible?"

"Terrible? It is...*amazing.*" My eyes crossed as she took me into her mouth again. *A blow job*, she'd said. I'd read about such things, but while reading about it, I'd thought it was strange. We had no such act in our old world. Having Cherry doing it to me was mind altering. Not strange at all —wonderful!

She stroked the bottom of my cock with her tongue and sucked and stroked the rest of me with her mouth while one of her hands wrapped around my shaft. I watched as her full lips dragged along my dick. I would not be able to withstand much more.

"Cherry, stop."

She pulled away and pouted at me. "Sorry. It's no good, is it?"

I shook my head, in awe. "No...no. I mean yes! Yes! It is good. It is very, very good! I have never felt such pleasure."

She tilted her head to the side and made a face. "What do you mean?"

"That…I…it does not matter. I am grateful. You have honored me by giving me such pleasure. But I have other plans for you." To show her what I meant, I lifted her into my arms and kissed her, tasting the mix of the both of us as our tongues tangled. "I wish to mate you properly. I wish to enter you."

She shivered and nodded her head. "Yes, please."

Something about the way my pretty little mate said *please* spoke to my baser dragon instincts, spurring a surge of animalistic frenzy.

My arms tightened around her and I clamped my mouth on her neck, sucking the tender skin over her pulsing vein. "Say please again," I growled.

Her nails scored my back and her body quivered against mine, her hard nipples brushed over my chest hair. "Cezar… *pleeeease*."

I pushed her back on the bed and moved over her. Bracing myself on my arms, looking down at her, I felt my world shift. I would have given the female beneath me anything in the world, and *she* was begging for *me*. My dragon demanded that I take her hard and fast—mark her, sink my teeth into her tender skin and lick away the droplets of blood that spilled.

But, she was delicate and I put all my focus into reining in my true nature to appease hers. I forced myself to slow down and take my time, trailing kisses over her neck and shoulders, ravishing her breasts with my tongue, rolling her nipples between my lips. and nibbling at her rib cage until she begged me again. It was a slow, exquisite torture for both of us.

"Please, in me. In me, now." Cherry flung her head back and forth, writhing under me, her soft curves rubbing up against me.

I kissed back up to her mouth and held her gaze. "Assure me that you want this."

"I want this. Please."

Kissing her, I slowly guided my shaft into her. She was so tight, I thought I'd die before I was fully inside of her. Cherry's sweet core milked me, her pulse raced, her breathing became erratic as I slid farther into her, inch by inch. She wrapped her arms and legs around me, locking on, and moaned into my kiss. Halfway in, I couldn't take it anymore. I pushed hard and broke the rest of the way in, in one stroke. I moaned in pleasure as my world narrowed to the female beneath me on that bed. *My* female.

Cherry broke away from the kiss and sank her teeth into my shoulder, muffling a scream. Her core throbbed around me and her body flooded with even more of her natural juices as she came.

The bite of her small, blunt-tipped teeth set me off. I withdrew my shaft slowly and thrust back in quickly, burying it again. I gripped her ass in one hand, holding her still while I pistoned in and out. The sweet nectar of her orgasm, the scent of our copulating permeating the room, was more intoxicating than any brew of Armand's. Yet, I needed more. I didn't stop until I was hearing her scream my name, urging me—begging me—not to stop while I sucked and kissed her breasts and then the skin of her neck where I longed to mark her. I desperately wanted her to wear my claiming mark, but I knew she wasn't ready. So, I settled on sucking on her skin, marking her the way a human mate might do.

Cherry's body clenched around me again and again, meeting my cock with a deliciously tight squeeze every time I plunged into her. When she kissed me, she nibbled, her teeth biting down on my lower lip and then she pulled back to gaze into my eyes. The heat and desire in her gaze was the most beautiful thing I'd ever seen. She bit her bottom lip when I shifted my hips and entered her at a different angle, stroking her in a higher place, a place that set her off again. A place that I would commit to memory. "Yes, Cezar!"

I couldn't help the proud grin I flashed before lowering my mouth to hers. Pleasure built in me, higher and higher, until I could feel my entire body tighten. I wanted her to orgasm again, with me, so I reached between us and brushed my fingers over her little button of nerves.

Cherry bit my lip, accidentally that time, and dug her nails into my back. Her walls tightened around me until I wasn't sure I could move another inch, and then she screamed my name in a way I'd longed to hear my entire life. I watched the chords of muscle in her throat work, clenching and releasing, as she screamed. My entire body stilled with that sight and my seed released into her in hot throbbing jets.

I buried my face between her breasts and scraped my teeth along her tightly puckered chocolate nipples. I wanted so desperately to mark her. Instead, I dug my fingers into the sheets beside her head. A part of my soul found its home in Cherry.

We both stayed where we were, trembling and holding onto each other. I wasn't sure how much time had passed, but I was still hard and she was probably sore. I wanted her again, but I had already been rougher than I'd intended. My priority was to care for her and I could wait.

But, when I tried to pull out of her, Cherry moaned softly and stroked her hand down my back to cup my ass. I lifted my head and studied her as she gazed back up at me, a sort of awe-filled confusion in her eyes as they moved over my face. That look was quickly replaced by lust.

"I fear that I might hurt you, Cherry."

Her slick, tight core squeezed me and her already flushed cheeks burned brighter. "You're still hard."

"Because, you are the sexiest female I have ever seen."

She rolled her eyes but gasped when I cupped her chin and rocked my hips against hers. She tried to look away, but I held her steady. "What—"

"You don't believe me."

"No."

I rolled us over and groaned when her sweet thighs settled on either side of my hips. "Then I will prove it to you."

13

CHERRY

I gripped the book tighter in my hands and stared blindly across the library and into thin air. Something didn't make sense to me and I was determined to figure it out. I could still picture Cezar's face from the night before, slowly changing and morphing even as I watched. Golden veins had appeared under his skin; his green eyes had glowed an even brighter green, and even his teeth had seemed to increase in length. Not just his teeth. I was still sore and walking with a slight hitch to my step because, as if he wasn't big enough already, when he got closer to orgasming, his shaft had grown, too. It all sounded completely crazy, or it would have if I hadn't been there to witness it for myself. But I had been and I knew what I saw. And felt.

I probably should have been freaked out or scared, but the whole thing had been so beautiful. Even as his skin rippled with what looked like green scales, I was entranced by him. I hadn't been able to stop needing more, either. He indulged me two more times before he'd refused because he could already see the way I moved was achy and stiff. I'd been like a fiend. A nympho. Which was maybe the oddest thing of all since sex wasn't something that I'd ever really cared about before. I'd certainly never craved it to nymphomaniacal heights.

I'd always heard that the first time was supposed to be awkward and uncomfortable. Nothing about sex with Cezar could be described that way. And I just couldn't get enough of him.

I forced myself to look back down at the book. As I skimmed the pages, I wasn't even sure what I was looking for or where to find it. I was holding a cheap shifter romance novel, something we didn't even keep on the library shelves. It was from one of my bookcases at home. I'd grabbed it before running out that morning. I knew it was crazy, but I had this theory…well, something about Cezar hadn't been *normal,* I was certain. I turned pages and looked for clues in the sex scenes of the book. Maybe, he wasn't even human.

"What are you up to?"

I jumped about a foot in the air and gasped. Chyna stood in front of me, wearing a smug smirk simply because she'd been able to sneak up and startle me. I quickly shut the book and put it under the desk. "N-nothing. What are you doing here? Shouldn't you be out rescuing plants?"

She appraised me with a curious eye. "Something's different about you."

I shook my head. "Nope. Nothing. Nothing is different."

"Yeah, there is something. I can't put my finger on it. It's there, though. It's not a haircut… Did you change something?"

"Why aren't you on a scavenger hunt for a lost species of pteridophytes, Chyna?"

"Do you even know what I do?"

I grinned. "Sure. I know the title you hold."

She rolled her eyes then continued to look me up and down. "I'll figure out what's different about you. For now, though, I have more research to do."

I watched her walk off and did a quick scan of the room. There were plenty of people in the library for a Saturday morning. Things were going well; no one seemed to need any help. The only person who seemed uneasy was me.

I went back over everything I knew about and every interaction I'd had with Cezar. My conclusion was that guys that looked like they should play the leading man in big screen blockbuster romances didn't just show up out of the blue and fall for a nerdy, disheveled librarian. Nor did they shower said librarian with expensive gifts, beg said librarian to date them, or proceed to bestow multiple orgasms upon said librarian. I knew all this to be fact. I mean, I hadn't stayed a virgin until the age of twenty-nine for moral reasons.

I pulled the book back out and stared down at it again. Maybe I was losing my grip on reality. I rolled my shoulders. I'd been stressed lately, hadn't I? Life had been a little more intense than normal, with the promotion and everything. Was it possible that I was experiencing stress-induced psychosis? I'd read about such a thing occurring. It made more sense than the idea of shifters being real. Although, the idea of Cezar not being real was more than a little depressing.

Fire Breathing Cezar

As though my thoughts had conjured him out of thin air, Cezar suddenly appeared at the circulation desk. I jumped and threw the book behind me. "Hey."

He smiled and raised a brow. "What did that poor book ever do to you?"

"Nothing!" I forced a smile and took a couple steps back, away from him. What if he wasn't really standing there? What if he was just a figment of my overstressed, overworked mind? "Stay here. I've got to do something."

Before he could protest, I rounded the desk and was hurrying into the back room Chyna liked to use for her research. *Here goes nothin'*. I stood in front of her with my hands on my hips trying to appear calm, rational and, most of all, sane. "I need help."

She nodded. "I've known that for years."

"Hardy-har-har. I need your help with something right now." I pulled her arm. "Right now."

She sighed and stood up. "What do you want?"

I pulled her to the doorway and pointed at the desk where Cezar stood waiting. "Do you see anyone at the circulation desk?"

She scrunched her face into a look that confirmed that I'd lost my mind. "What are you getting at?"

I pointed harder. "The desk. Do you *see* anyone? I'm serious, Chyna."

"Yes. I see that hottie that was here a while back. The one who sent you the gazillion gifts. What's up, Cherry?"

I slumped against the door. "You *see* him?"

"Jesus, Cherry. Yes, I see him. He's not invisible. Are you okay?" She put her hand to my forehead, but I batted it away.

"I'm fine. I just..." I pulled her back into the room this time, plopped onto one of the chairs and blew out a slow breath. "I slept with him."

She squealed. "No way!"

I nodded. "Exactly! That's exactly what I mean! It doesn't make sense. There's no way that *he'd* want to sleep with *me*. Look at him. Look at me. I—"

"Hey, what the hell? What do you mean *look at you*? You're beautiful. Any man in his right mind would want you."

I slid my glasses down my nose and looked over the rims at her. "Chyna, I'm not blind. You're the pretty twin. I'm the plain, nerdy twin. It's fine. I accept that. But I, nerdy librarian, slept with a man who looks like Mr. Hollywood blockbuster. I mean, what's his agenda?!"

I might've yelled that last part. Loud enough that the normal low hum of the library faded to nothing. Nothing but footsteps coming our way. I knew whose they were before I even looked up.

He stepped into the room, grinning from ear to ear. "Mr. Hollywood, at your service."

Chyna giggled and I wanted to smack her. "I'm Cherry's sister, Chyna."

Cezar shook her hand and then stepped beside me. He wrapped an arm around me and pulled me to my feet lowering his mouth to my ear. "As much as I love hearing you proclaim to the world that we are sleeping together, I do not like hearing you say such things about yourself."

"What—"

"Also, I am the one who is grateful that you have honored me by sharing a bed with me. The only agenda I have is to try to be the male you deserve."

"She tends to over dramatize things from time to time." Chyna laughed and winked at me. I glared back at her. "Well, I'm going to get back to my work, if you two don't mind."

I was living someone else's life—a fictional character from a shifter romance novel. I couldn't exactly tell Chyna that I thought the hot guy who I'd let into my pants was some kind of shifter, and certainly not in front of him. Or maybe an alien. I hadn't thought of that. What if he was an alien?

I hadn't even made him wear a condom. Why hadn't I thought of safe sex? Sweet baby Jesus, what if he implanted me with his alien offspring? "I think I need some air."

Chyna nodded to Cezar. "I'm assuming you've got it covered? Considering the fact that you haven't let my sister go since the moment you set eyes on her?"

"I've got her."

The next thing I knew, I was being led outside through the back door of the library by someone I was convinced was of an alien race. I was dizzy, breathing heavily—hyperventilating. I was probably already impregnated by his alien seed and it was mere hours before I started to show.

The parking lot. We were in the parking lot and it was spinning. I remembered the movie *Alien* with Sigourney Weaver. How long did I have before an alien baby popped out of my chest cavity like some sort of bloody, razor-fanged jack in the box?

We'd barely made it outside the building when I felt the world shift beneath my feet. That was it. *It's already happening*, I thought as the world went black.

14

CHERRY

I awoke to muffled sounds, strange scents and white circles. Circular shapes. It was a ceiling. I was staring at a ceiling that had a white circular patterning. My head felt heavy as I lifted it off the pillow and looked around. I was in what looked like a chic, contemporary showroom. The walls were floor to ceiling glass panels. The floor was white and beige marble and the elegant furniture was off-white with accents of navy and burgundy. A large, white marble spiral staircase led to an upper floor. Light poured into the space through the massive windows, so I knew it was still daytime, and outside was the most incredible view of the swampy wetlands of the Louisiana bayou country.

I stood up. The kitchen was open to the rest of the house, well, it was somewhat walled off but the walls were a thick, clear glass. Cezar was on the other side of the glass, standing at a kitchen island with a knife and a tomato in his hand.

He glanced up at me just as I began moving in his direction. His lips started to curve into a smile, then fell. His eyes widened as his gaze dropped to something in front of me. Puzzled, I looked down just in time to keep myself from stepping into a swimming pool. I gasped and took a step back. Jeez, a swimming pool right in the room! Maybe it was supposed to be an indoor pond or something, but no wonder I'd missed it. It looked like clear, blue glass. I had thought it was part of the solid flooring. The place was too much.

When I looked back, Cezar was no longer holding the knife, but his finger was covered in dripping blood. I quickly rounded the pool, or pond, whatever, and rushed over to him.

"Cezar, are you okay?" I gently took his hand and pulled him over to the sink. "That looks painful."

He stood behind me, letting me hold his finger under a stream of water, but he didn't seem to feel any pain at all. In fact, he wasn't paying a bit of attention to his injured finger. He ran his nose up my neck and lightly moaned. "You smell so delicious."

I glanced back at him and froze. His gaze was intense. His eyes were glowing and he was completely aroused. I knew this because his rock-hard erection was pressing into my lower back.

"I apologize. I should not be acting like an animal when you are recovering from a fainting spell. You frightened me."

I dropped my head to focus on his injured finger, feeling a little embarrassed and self-conscious, but then I saw that the cut was gone. I turned his hand over in mine, back and forth. No cut anywhere. "What... Where did it go?"

Cezar frowned. "There is something we must discuss."

The whole alien thing popped back into my head along with the fear and panic. How had I forgotten the alien impregnation? Pushing him away, I raced to the other side of the room, flattened myself against the wall and shook my head. "You just healed yourself. You're an alien whose mission it is to abduct me, enslave me and transport me to your planet as a breeder to propagate your alien race, aren't you? Aren't you?! I knew it! Why me? Why pick me? It's because of the child bearing hips, isn't it?"

Cezar wrinkled his brow in confusion and took a step closer to me. "What are you talking about, Cherry? I would not abduct or enslave you."

"Which is *exactly* what an alien who wanted to abduct me would say! I can't believe I gave up my virginity to a human-abducting alien. I'll never live this down."

"Dragon, Cherry. I am a dragon."

I stopped rambling and looked at him. "Huh?"

He took another step closer. "I am a *dragon*."

Without thinking, I snapped, "Prove it."

He ran his palms down his face, then shrugged and threw his hands in the air. "Okay. Outside."

I followed him out to a large marble courtyard that overlooked the swamp. The nature surrounding the place was beautiful—wild and untouched, raw. I found myself wishing I could stay for a while, even if he did turn out to be a human-abducting alien.

Cezar methodically undressed and turned to face me. "Are you prepared? I do not wish to watch you faint again."

"I think so. I've never been about to see a dragon before, though, so I'm not quite sure how to ready myself for it."

I'd barely gotten the words out when he ran to the edge of the courtyard and leapt into the air. Like magic, Cezar disappeared and in his place was a massive green creature—a dragon covered with golden-tipped emerald green scales. His massive wings unfurled and the undersides of them glittered with gold. He soared higher into the air, and then, he tipped his head back and released a spray of fire so hot it burned blue.

I stood staring up, mouth agape. *Dragon.* He really was a fucking dragon. What was equally astonishing was how my body reacted to seeing the dragon...aroused. I gasped and backed away, like my outrage would somehow make the situation normal.

Cezar, the dragon, swooped down and hovered over the swamp next to me. He lowered his head and then turned to looked at me.

"What?"

He puffed out a little burst of fire and then made a sound that reminded me of laughter. He waved his head up and down and then nodded it towards his back. When I still didn't get it, he sunk down and slightly immersed himself in the water, then nudged me with his massive head and waited, still staring unblinkingly.

"What is it? What are you trying to say? When I figured it out, I shook my head emphatically and held my hands up.

"I'm *not* riding you. I'm human and you're a dragon. This girl's feet belong right here on terra firma."

He sent another little burst of fire at me and huffed.

"Hey, mister, if you burn me, I won't magically heal."

I could've sworn he rolled his eyes before he nodded towards me and then his back again.

I still shook my head, but slower. "Come on, ... I can't ride you."

He flapped his wing and with a skilled precision sent a wave of water at me. I didn't dodge it in time and the water splashed my legs. Another laughing sound and I was stomping towards him. I wagged my finger in his face and was about to tell him off when he bumped me with his head. Nudging me again and again until, somehow, I was on his back and he was taking off into the air with me holding on for dear life.

Terrifying at first, I found myself relaxing and enjoying it more and more. The longer he flew us over the wetland around his home, the more thrilled I was at the adventure I was experiencing. I was settled firmly at the base of his neck with my legs wrapped around him. I had loosened up pretty quickly after getting settled and I could feel the beat of his heart pulsing out a rhythm at the juncture between my thighs. Between the steady throbbing against my core and the thrill of being so high up in the air—and on a *dragon's* back, no less—I was having an amazing time.

I couldn't remember the last time I'd had such a blast. When he dipped and soared higher, I threw back my head in a fit of giggles. I felt like I was on a roller coaster. I never wanted it to end. "Faster!"

Another one of those dragon chuffing laughs and Cezar did as I'd demanded. He flew faster and even low enough to dip his wings into the water and splash us with a spray of droplets.

I held onto his neck tighter and laughed out loud at the craziness of it all. By the time he landed and shifted back, I was so energized and exhilarated and stimulated that I could barely walk. I was horny as hell.

The very second he morphed back into a hot hunky naked man, I jumped into his arms wrapping my legs around his hips. He must've felt that I was all hot and bothered because my clothes became tatters of cloth strewn across the courtyard floor before I could blink. His shaft penetrated me just as fast and we coupled like that, with him holding me in the air and filling me hard and fast. We both came in minutes.

Later, after were both sated and lying side by side on the couch in the gorgeous mansion that he referred to as his castle, his fingers gently stroking my shoulder, I looked over at him and sighed. "A dragon, huh?"

He trailed his finger down my stomach and dipped into my bellybutton before trailing back up. "You are not displeased?"

I laughed. "Well. I thought you were an alien before so, I suppose a dragon is much better."

"Damn right."

I rolled toward him and dug my face into his chest inhaling his dark, heady, masculine scent. Displeased? Who could be displeased with him. He was amazing. Even more amazing than my own histrionic imagination could concoct. Handsome, wealthy, a master in the sack, and a supernatural creature that no one in their right mind would fuck with.

Now more than ever, I was sure we didn't belong together and it was time I ended this farce before my heart turned up shattered into a million pieces.

15

CHERRY

"You should've let him in." Chyna admonished from her spot in the chair across from my bed. "He sounded worried."

I winced as I dabbed at my sore, red nose with a tissue. "Looking like this?" I waved a hand down the length of my body which was clad in an old T-shirt and faded yoga pants. Oh, and two pairs of thick, fluffy socks. "It's already crazy to pretend that Mr. Hollywood actually wants to be with someone like me. No way am I letting him see me like this."

I was sick and using it as an excuse to put distance between us. After spending the most amazing day ever together, Cezar had wanted me to stay over at his...ahem...castle, but I figured why prolong the inevitable and instead asked him to fly me home. Once we arrived, I'd told him that I needed some space. The truth was that I was hoping he'd get the hint and go on his merry hot way so I could continue on with my mundane existence.

"Cherry, what is up with you? I've never heard you be so down on yourself."

"You've also never seen a man as hot as Cezar showing interest in me. Or any man for that matter. It doesn't make any sense. Not even an average Joe pays any attention to women like me, much less a guy who's so hot he could have any woman he wants eating out of his hand. And he's sweet. He's funny, too. He's so... *amazing*, and I'm just...me, a weird introverted bookworm. I don't trust it. There must be some underlying motive. Why else would he be paying so much attention to me? It doesn't make any sense."

"What?! Cherry, you're beautiful. You're smart, sweet, and funny, too. And what you call weird, some call unique. Uniqueness is a wonderful trait. I think he'd be crazy to not want you."

"Come on, Chyna." I shook my head. "You only say stuff like that because you're my sister."

"I don't lie. You know that. I wouldn't say it if it wasn't true."

"Uh huh. You'd tell your only sister that she was dumb, dull and ugly? Right."

Chyna hesitated. "Well...if she was I might. BUT SHE'S NOT!"

I tried to laugh but it turned into a hacking cough. "It's just... I can't make sense of it and I don't like that. I feel like it's got to be a joke or something."

Chyna's face fell. "Do you really think he has no feelings for you? That he's trying to get you to fall for him so once you do he can pull the rug out from under you and say, 'Surprise, just kidding. It was all just a hoax.'? Do you really think that?"

I blew my nose and pouted. "No, I guess not. Not unless he's *really* good at pretending."

"The sex was that good, huh?"

I laughed up another coughing spell. Until I finished, Chyna lightly rubbed my back and hummed a song we used to sing to comfort one another when we were kids. When my coughing fit ended, I rested my head on her shoulder and sighed.

"Yeah, the sex was *that* good."

She grinned down at me and stroked my hair. "If you know it's real, why are you fighting it?"

"I told you. He's too special for me. Why try to make something work with him when it's bound to end with me being proven to be right? Then, he'll find someone as perfect as he is—some perfect supermodel or something and they'll go off and have perfect kids in his perfect home with their perfect life. There's no use courting heartbreak."

Chyna stiffened. "What did you say?"

"I said a lot. Do you really want me to repeat it all?"

She shook her head. "You said, 'There's no use courting heartbreak'. Why did you say that?"

I shrugged. "I don't know. 'Cause it's true?"

"You realize that that awful woman at the children's home used to say that to us, right?" She pushed my head off her shoulder and grasped me by the upper arms looking into my eyes. "That old witch that was there every time we had to go back between foster homes? Mrs. Harold or Harris or something like that? She said that to us. All the time."

I frowned. "Okay?"

"Come on, Cherry. You're an intelligent woman. Put it two and two together. Remember every time there was the possibility of us finding a forever family? When potential adopters would come in to see all of us, and we'd puff up like little birds. Remember when we used to dream about having a mom and dad who would let us help decorate the Christmas tree and give us chore lists and ground us when we got bad report cards? She would always tell us the same thing—over and over—that there was no use courting heartbreak, because out of all the available kids, no one in their right mind would ever pick two little brown-skinned girls whose own mama tossed them out like trash."

I stared up at the ceiling and blinked back tears. "That's not what this is about."

"Are you sure? Because it feels an awful lot like it to me. You keep acting like you're not good enough for him, so no matter how hard that man tries to convince you otherwise, you're not even going to give him a chance. You literally said the exact phrase she used to use, Cherry."

I sat up and scooted myself back against the headboard. "It's just a phrase, Chyna. I don't believe anything that old nasty witch said to us. I never did. She was just cruel and evil and unhappy with her own miserable existence."

Chyna shook her head, her eyes shining with unshed tears. "We both knew she was miserable and just trying to get us to join her in her misery, but we also both believed her. Even if just a little bit. She got to us and I am not going to let that old bitch ruin your chance at happiness. I refuse." Chyna wiped the back of her hand over her cheeks swiping at the tears that were now streaming down her face. "Get up. We're going to go find him." She tugged my arm and started yanking me out of my bed. She was strong for her size and I was halfway off the bed and almost on the floor before I snapped.

"Stop! I'm serious when I say he's too amazing. He's a dragon! That's how fucking special he is, Chyna. He can literally turn into a two-hundred-ton creature and fly through the sky. Scales, wings, talons, the whole nine yards."

She stopped pulling me and frowned. "Oh, honey, I think your fever has spiked."

"No, no. Listen to me." I paused and ran a hand through my nappy hair wincing as it got caught in the tangles. "He really is a dragon, Chyna, I saw it. He transformed into one for me. Then, he flew me over the swamp while I hung onto his neck."

"You're delirious."

I nodded. "Yeah. I mean, no. I'm not hallucinating. I also saw him cut his finger and it healed itself—in seconds. I saw his eyes glow and golden veins appear from beneath his skin. I know it sounds crazy, but I swear to you, Chyna, it's all true."

She rubbed her hands down her face. "A *dragon*? As in a mythical creature of medieval folklore and legend?"

"Yup. The very same. Except these guys haven't been here that long and they're actually from another planet."

She nodded, the corner of her mouth upturned like she was about to take out her phone and record me so she could post a viral video of the crazy things I said while in a state of delirium. "Which planet?"

"Which pl—? I don't know! You're missing the point. You know those romance books about shape shifters? Bears, lions, wolves, yadda, yadda."

"You're saying he's a shapeshifter? A *dragon* shifter?"

We were quiet for a while and I still wasn't exactly sure she believed me. Then she looked over at me and laughed so hard she fell on the floor clutching her stomach. When she finished, she took a few moments to catch her breath. "You lost your virginity to a dragon shifter?"

I rolled my eyes. "Think that's bad? At first I thought he was an alien trying to abduct me and take me to his planet as a breeding slave to further his alien species."

She snorted. "No."

"Yep. I accused him of impregnating me because I have child bearing hips."

"*No!*"

"Mm-hmm."

Again, silence fell around us and we both sat there, lost in our own thoughts. I didn't know what Chyna was thinking but I was remembering a sad little girl who, for her own survival, was forced to wall off the part of her heart that contained innocent, wide-eyed vulnerability and the crazy notion that she was worthy of love simply because she existed. The girl who was never special enough to get picked but was weird—unique—enough to get picked on.

Had that sad little girl had grown into a sad, lonely woman whose heart was imprisoned in its own high tower? Perhaps, but why shouldn't it be? For protection. Just because the years had passed, did that mean the cards I'd been dealt would magically change?

No, it wasn't just what some mean and stupid old woman said to us when we were kids. It was the way everything in my life transpired. The way everything had always transpired. It had always been just Chyna and me. She was my safety net and I was hers, and we didn't need anyone else.

Besides, the new page I had wanted to turn had been turned and I accomplished the goal of having my cherry popped (pun intended).

It was time to close the book on that chapter.

16

CEZAR

I did not understand my human mate. She was excited when she learned I was a dragon. Of that, I was certain. She laughed as she rode on my back. She even became aroused. I thought that I had finally pleased her, yet she refused to remain with me at my castle and demanded that I take her home. I begged her to talk to me and to allow me to make amends for whatever it was I had done to displease her.

I could scent her sorrow, yet she would not discuss it with me. She simply told me that she needed *space* and asked that I respect her wishes and leave her alone. This was a human thing, the needing of *space*. I had read about it and did not like it at all. Not one bit. However, I had little choice.

When I found that she was ill, I tried to go to her home and check on her, but she refused to allow me to see her. I knew she was ill because she did not go to work at the library, and I knew that because as far as giving her *space* was concerned, I could do it none other than the dragon way. Which meant that I remained covertly nearby every minute.

I'd had to cancel a gaming marathon with Nick and Casey, but the younglings were understanding when I explained I had found my mate but was having difficulty winning her over and that it was taking every minute of my time.

I was becoming distraught. I'd done everything the books recommended, yet I was hiding like a coward, for fire's sake! Worse, from what the books said, "I need space" was a phrase used by humans to sometimes serve as a kind and gentle way of ending a relationship. I did not find it gentle or kind. Nor would I allow us to end. I could not and I would not.

∼

****Cherry****

I was bedridden with the flu for three days. The worst part, as much as I hated to admit it, was that I couldn't stop thinking about Cezar. It appeared as though putting space between us was not going to be easy. So far, it was much harder being away from him than it was being with him. My first day back was spent playing catch up, but I was also feeling a bit sad that Cezar hadn't fought harder for me—for us. Which was the damned dumbest thing ever since I was the one who kept metaphorically kicking him in the nuts to get him to go. I suppose it had been my test of how hard I had to push him before he ended up leaving.

Not very hard, it would seem.

As I wallowed in the mire of my own making, a woman and two teenaged boys came up to the front desk. The woman asked for me by name. I attempted to give her the pleasantest smile I could muster, but it probably looked more like a pained half-grin.

"Yes, I'm Cherry Deschamps. How can I help you?"

She took in a deep breath and blew it out slowly. "Um, hello. My name is Sky Broussard and this is Nick." She pointed to a tall boy in about his mid-teens, and then to another who was maybe a year or two younger. "And Casey."

"Nice to meet y'all." We all stared at one another in silence for several seconds as I waited for someone to say something. I didn't know where this was going, but in the south, we didn't like to rush things. Besides, I had all the time in the world since my social calendar was likely to be completely clear from now until forever.

"Spit it out, Sky." The younger of the two boys rolled his eyes and then looked at me. "Cezar told us about you."

I felt a burn creep up my cheeks. "Oh..."

Sky smacked him on the arm and pushed him away. "Go look for some books to check out."

The taller boy leaned towards me. "Cezar is awesome and he really likes you. He's a great guy and we think you should cut him a break."

Sky groaned and shoved him away from the desk. "I am so sorry about that. Is there somewhere we could speak privately?"

I stuttered and nearly tripped over myself getting around the desk. "Y-yes. In my office."

She followed behind me and pushed the door closed once we were inside. "I'm sorry to just show up like this unannounced and butt into your business and all." She held her hands up in front of her as she spoke. "It's really not my place, so if you want to tell me to buzz off, I get it. I just thought maybe I could help—offer a friendly shoulder or something—since I've been exactly where you are."

I dropped into my desk chair and held my breath. What did she mean *exactly where I was*? And then it dawned on me. She must be Cezar's ex. Or, one of his exes, perhaps. Oh, god, are those boys out there his children? Jealousy reared its ugly head and I found myself comparing my physical attributes to hers. We were oddly similarly shaped, although she may have been slightly curvier than I was.

I narrowed my eyes suspiciously. "You've been exactly where I am in what way?"

"Well, I was stuck between falling head over heels and wanting to run away screaming at the top of my lungs." She sighed. "Not to mention my knowledge of the universe having to expand to include things I'd only ever thought were figments of the twisted imaginations of fiction writers."

She hadn't confirmed or denied my suspicions, so I decided to just come out and ask what I really wanted to know. "Were you and Cezar... Are you and Cezar..." It was harder than I thought to get the words out. *Deep breath*. "How are you and your boys related to Cezar? Are you his ex?"

"No! Lord ha' mercy, no! We're not related. Well, Nick and Casey and I are...but not to Cezar. The boys are my nephews. Cezar is my mate's...uh...brother—friend—brother. They're, you know, similar."

"Your *mate*?"

"Goodness, chère, Has Cezar told you nothing?"

I was starting to feel like I was in an alternate universe. "I guess not."

"Well, he told us that you know about his, ahem, other form? I'm assuming you know that, or this is about to get really awkward."

As though it wasn't already. "I know about the dragon."

"Okay, but he didn't mention mates?"

I shook my head.

"I see. Well, then." She cleared her throat and seemed to be considering her words before she continued. "Dragons have mates. And, until they find their mate, they spend most of their lives searching for her. It's this odd thing like something in their chemical makeup finds a person, a mate, whose chemical makeup is extremely compatible with theirs and, once they find them, that's it."

"What do you mean that's it?"

"Their dragon recognizes her as its mate and latches on. Then, they will only be attracted to that person and no other from that moment on. I'm not really sure how it works on a scientific level or anything, but I can assure you that it does work. I guess it's what we humans would call soulmates. When they find their soulmate, they know instantaneously, like Cezar knew with you, and then, apparently, they run around in a whirlwind of lunacy acting like damn fools and possessive Neanderthals who beat their chests with their fists and all but club you and throw you over their shoulder."

I blinked at her. "What?"

She laughed and fanned herself. "Sorry, I'm all over the place. I'm remembering my own experiences. I've only known about dragons for a little while. I'm just a normal person like you. A waitress, actually. I was so shocked and amazed, but I thought that Beast and I...Beast is my mate. I thought that we didn't make sense. I even told him that I couldn't be with him. I was certain, in fact. But, I was so wrong.

"I came over here hoping to save you the heartache I went through. But, at this moment I wonder if I'm only managing to sound crazier and crazier the more I keep flapping my gums."

I cleared my throat and twisted a strand of hair nervously around my finger. "So, Cezar asked you to come over here?"

"Oh, no, no. He doesn't know I'm here. This was my idea. Even though we're virtually strangers, I feel a strange kind of connection to you seeing as how we're both mates of dragons."

"I...I think you've gotten mixed up somehow. I am not Cezar's soulmate."

Sky's face froze. "Of course you are."

I shook my head and wished away the blush burning my cheeks. "No. I haven't even seen the guy in days." Of course, I didn't tell her that that was due in part to the fact that I'd told him to go take a flying leap. Not in those exact words, of course.

"No, that's not right. Dragons are possessive and demanding. Beast followed me around and wouldn't leave, hung out at my workplace, even marked me without permission. He's behaving now, but we had some issues to iron out over that uber-possessiveness."

"Now I know you have the wrong person." I stood up and hurried to my office door to usher her out before I did something silly like cry or something. "Cezar isn't like that with me at all."

She looked truly perplexed. "He talks about you, though. You're definitely his mate. I'm not mistaken about that."

"If I was his…soulmate, or mate, whatever, then why hasn't he been around in days?" I blinked back tears. "Why doesn't he behave the way you say he's supposed to? The whole possessive Neanderthal and throwing over the shoulder thing."

She stood up and pulled her purse strap over her shoulder. "I've obviously upset you and I'm so sorry. Cezar and my mate are a little different, maybe that's it. I mean, Cezar's the diplomat of the group, a little more civilized than the rest, I guess. I do know you're his mate, though. Please don't cry, chère. I made things worse and it was truly not my intention. I'm so sorry. I'll go. Here, let me give you my number. Call me if you need anything. I promise I'll try not to make you cry next time."

I watched her go and then stayed in my office feeling sorry for myself. I had made the choice to keep Cezar and all men out of my life, so I couldn't really blame him. But what she said cut deep. Whoever turned out to be Cezar's soulmate was going to be one luck girl. Especially if he did throw her over his shoulder and follow her around and hang out at her workplace and, what else had she said? Mark her without permission? Whatever that meant.

I remembered the tsunami of gifts Cezar showered me with. Sure, that had been something, but he'd also made himself scarce easily enough. As soon as I'd said I needed space, he'd backed right off. And why wouldn't he? I had been nothing but a plaything to him, something to bide his time until he found this "soulmate" of his. Besides, I still found it way too difficult to believe that a man as fine as Cezar would have a connection like Sky described to someone like me and, regardless of what my sister said, to think otherwise was courting heartache.

My office door opened again minutes later and the older of Sky's nephews stood there, looking awkward. "Hi. Uh, I just wanted to say that Cezar isn't the best at dating or whatever. He's old. Super old. It makes him kind of clueless. I know you're his mate, though. He called you his mate. He told me you were."

I wiped my eyes and smiled at the boy. "Thanks for trying."

The boy rocked back and forth on his feet, clearly not wanting to leave without getting his point across. "One time Beast almost ripped a man's head off for looking at Sky too long. Maybe if you don't believe it, all you have to do is have another man show interest in you or treat you poorly." With that, he smiled sheepishly and turned to leave, reconsidered, and turned aback around. "You'll want to be careful with that, though. He's from a species of battle-hardened warrior creatures who can char a dude to cinders and then consume his ashes. See ya'." At that, he left me to consider his words like they were some credo passed down from the gods of Olympus.

It was tempting. No, it wasn't. It was stupid. So stupid. Why would I take the advice of a child when it came to something like my love life? Or lack of love life, to be more specific. I already knew what I knew. He would've made some bigger show of having me be his, apparently. Maybe ripped a man's head off to really show me. Instead, he'd disappeared. After I demanded he leave and pushed him away, to be fair, but *still*. If someone truly wanted you the way Sky had described, they wouldn't just leave no matter how hard you pushed them away.

What did it even matter? I didn't want to be his stupid mate, anyway. I didn't want to be anyone's mate. Just call me Single Sally. Which was, incidentally, much better sounding than Solitary Cherry.

17

CEZAR

I spent what felt like years keeping myself at arms length and watching my mate from afar. It was actually only a week. I had seen Sky and the younglings visit the library the previous evening and did not expect that they had arrived there by coincidence. I hoped that perhaps Sky had been able to pacify Cherry's reservations. I was aching to discover if she was more favorable to mating but I had also promised to give her *space*. While I didn't know the length of time *space* required, I vowed to wait an entire week before showing myself again.

As the week ended, I was yearning to reunite with my mate. I flew home to shower and dress, hoping to present myself in a nicer than normal fashion, but my entire wardrobe consisted of jeans and T-shirts, so I simply settled for clothing without holes.

It was nearing closing time and rather than flying, I drove my truck to the library. I was hoping that perhaps Cherry might allow me to take her to dinner or a movie after she

Fire Breathing Cezar 109

closed up the library. I did not exactly understand how staying away from one another for a week was supposed to help, but I assumed my lack of understand of such things was due to the fact that I was not human.

As I stepped through the library doors, I was completely unprepared for the assault on my senses and the subsequent reaction of my body. The moment I opened the door and stepped inside, Cherry's scent was everywhere, permeating the room. That, combined with the fact that I hadn't been able to fuck my mate and had spent the week longing for her from afar, sent all the blood in my body to my dick, turning it to steel. I was so hard, that I had to painfully make my way over and slide behind one of the cases of books to give myself time to allow my erection to subside. I wanted nothing more than to be buried in my mate. It took ten minutes of me forcing myself to envision Ovide's hairy ass while I breathed sparingly out of my mouth before I softened enough to be able to move.

When I had better control over my libido, I stepped out in search of Cherry. My eyes were immediately drawn to her. She stood next to the front desk wearing a bright yellow dress that made her complexion glow. It flowed around her thighs as she twisted to reach something behind her back. When she straightened, her body stiffened and she swung around locking eyes with me. I was hoping for a smile, a welcome, a kind greeting, but she turned her back on me without a word.

It was not the warm reception I was hoping for. Had I erred by presenting myself too soon? I hoped that *space* was not supposed to last for longer than a week. I was not certain I would survive much longer. I paused to consider how best to handle her chilly reception. It was then that I noticed the male beside her.

"Oh, you're so funny, Gary." Cherry was lightly resting her hand on his forearm and smiling up at him. My dragon arose. My eyes were glued to her hand on that male's arm. I fought to maintain control and keep my dragon subdued as I unsuccessfully tried to stifle a growl. I vaguely heard a few gasps from what I could only assume were others in the room.

Gary, lucky for him, did not react. He just nodded and flipped the book he held over his hands. "I think this will do it."

"Are you sure you don't need anything else?" Cherry was twirling a strand of hair around her finger as she batted her eyelashes at the soon to be dead male.

Gary just smiled and shook his head. "Thank you, Cherry. Appreciate your help."

I realized I was still emitting a low growl. I thought I'd stopped. My dragon was incensed, the threat to burn the place to the ground was real. He didn't care about anything but eliminating the threat—Gary—and claiming his mate.

Beast sounded in my head.

Brother, are you good? You are radiating fury through my head like a steam engine.

No, I am not. A male is too near my mate. I will kill him. After I rip his grinning head from his scrawny neck, I will shred his body and devour his innards.

There was silence for a while and then the sound of laughter.

You are behaving as I behaved with Sky. Do you remember how well my jealousy worked? I almost lost her. So much for trying to court your mate the human way!

I grabbed the side of a shelf to steady myself. He was right. I had to gain control of myself. I was driven by instinct—the need to assert my dominance, prove myself the worthier male, display my fighting prowess and willingness to die for my mate. If I behaved according to instinct, I would certainly lose any chance and destroy any progress I had made thus far.

I must react in the way a human male would. I needed to be a *gentle*male. When I did manage to close the gap between myself and Cherry, I still felt like a wild animal, more dragon than male. "Who is Gary?"

With red cheeks, Cherry frowned up at me. "I don't know what you're talking about."

"I saw you with the male you called Gary. I want to know if I have competition."

She went around to the other side of her desk and sat down. "You haven't been around in quite some time. I didn't know you were still interested."

"You told me to give you *space*."

"According to what Sky told me, dragons are possessive. I haven't seen or heard from you in a week. That says a whole lot, I think. Don't you?"

Possessive? I wanted to turn her over my knee and spank her ass red.

"What do you care if I was flirting with Gary? You wrote me off the minute I told you to give me space. You don't care about me. Why are you even here? All the other women in town busy, so you come running to Cherry to keep you company?"

My words froze on my tongue. I had so much to say, so much anger bouncing around, but I was stupefied by what she was implying. I opened my mouth to say something, but nothing came out.

"Exactly. You need to leave now. We're about to close." She turned away from me, cutting me off. She got up and stormed into her office, slamming the door behind her.

As much control as I was usually able to wield over my dragon, Cherry's words and actions had dissolved it to nil. A boiling rage simmered beneath my skin threatening an uncontrolled shift. I stood rooted to the spot willing my anger to cool, taking deep breaths, attempting to subdue the raging beast within. A puff of smoke hurled from my nostrils but I was too focused on not burning the place to cinders to notice whether or not any of the humans in the library saw it. It took several minutes before I was able to quell my dragon enough to safely leave the library.

I had given her *space* as she asked. It had been torturous, but I did it because she told me it was what she required. Yet, a week later, she was angry with me because I gave her *space*. She thought I did not care for her. I clearly did not understand how this human interaction was supposed to correctly transpire. It would appear that I had made every mistake that a firemouthed idiot could make. I was at my lowest point of despair.

Suppressing my own needs and instincts in order to claim my mate may indeed work eventually, but I was realizing that it was likely to kill me before it did.

18

CHERRY

I let Marilyn close down the library while I stayed hidden in my office. I was mortified and shamed by my behavior. What had I been thinking flirting with Gary? It had been a petty, childish thing to do and even if Cezar had reacted with jealousy, which he hadn't, it was still a low blow. I'd listened to a child and tried something sophomoric. My punishment was the shame I was feeling. Well, that and the pain of rejection. In fact, shame and pain were battling it out for supremacy.

I'd never done anything with a man before—no dating, no relationships, and certainly no deep feelings. I didn't understand the rules. But that was a piss poor excuse.

My other excuse was that I hadn't been able to employ my usual method of obtaining information which was to reference the self-help section of the library because, first of all, it had nothing on dragons, and, second of all, there wasn't even anything to look up. That stupid, childish little test of mine had proven that I wasn't Cezar's soulmate. His reaction had made it perfectly clear. According to Sky and her nephew, if I was, he would not have been so willing to turn me over to another man.

Besides, he hadn't shown up for a week. He hadn't even sent gifts or tried to call. Nothing. As I thought about it, though, I wasn't even sure he had a phone. I didn't know very much about him.

Ugh, I just needed to forget what I did know. It should've been easy enough. I mean, he was just a hot guy who had shown up, showered me with gifts, given me amazing orgasms, and then faded away.

I figured I should look at the bright side and take the experience for what it was. Who else got to say they lost their virginity to a handsome dragon who was a sex god? I'd just forget about him.

～

I spent that entire Sunday thinking about him. Living alone had always been fine with me. But I suddenly felt as though I was walking around an empty home with a huge hole through my center. As though half of me was missing and the other half was longing to reunite with it. I had never before felt so alone. Not to mention my continual state of arousal. My body ached. My nipples were constantly hard, my skin was so hypersensitive that the fabric of my clothing was scratchy, and it felt as though there was a constant drumbeat playing in my panties. None of it make any sense.

In the back of my mind, there was that thing Sky said about soulmates. Was that what was going on with me? What if I had been wrong in judging Cezar's reactions to mean that I wasn't his mate? I knew what I was feeling at that moment—like we were already somehow connected and had been destined before either of us ever met. *Whoa*. I was scaring myself. That was crazy talk.

I tried to think back to what Sky had said. How had she know? Had she felt the same way about her mate? I remembered her saying something about thinking that they didn't make sense and telling him that she couldn't be with him. I also remembered clear as day when she'd stated, "But, I was so wrong."

~

When I got to work Monday morning I was a prickly bitch. My hormones were through the roof, and I ached to be near Cezar, yet stubbornly, I refused to admit it, even to myself.

Cameron was working that morning and she made a face and shook her head when she saw me. "Girl, you look like something the cat dragged in. Rough weekend? Finally get that hot date?"

I took a deep breath in and tried to calm my temper before responding to her. It didn't work. I was usually so adept at letting thing roll off my back. I didn't like to make a fuss except, apparently, with Cezar. With him, I was all fuss and no roll off. But, today was not a good day to fuck with Cherry. Cherry wasn't into taking shit from anyone. I'd been letting Cameron's catty remarks slip by for years, but today I was sporting the mother of all PMS spells.

"Cameron, do me a favor."

She smiled and nodded. "What is it?"

"Keep your opinions of my love life and my appearance to your damned self. It's none of your damned business anyway, so shut it." I added a syrupy sweet smile.

My 'tude continued later when Slayer came in and lodged a formal complaint over the material in the book club. I didn't even know we had a formal complaint system. She'd had to show me where the paperwork was. As she berated me about the quality of the writing and the vulgarity of our readings, I listened with my arms crossed over my chest, waiting. She'd have to pause at some point and then I was going to politely tell her where she could shove it.

When the moment came, I smiled at her and held up my hand to hush her. "I appreciate your concern, I do. The book club has grown tremendously since we started these readings. Everyone loves Marilyn, including your friends. At least three of them told me that they loved what we were doing here. So, I'm sorry, but if you don't like it, I suggest you stay home and find something more suited to your tastes. Maybe a nice documentary on torture."

Her face burned red and she scribbled a few more lines on the complaint form before shoving it at my chest. Then she waved her knobby finger in my face and I noticed for the first time that she bore an uncanny resemblance to Almira Gulch from the *Wizard of Oz*. I wondered why I never noticed before. "I'm going to take this job back, missy. I made a mistake thinking that you could handle it. You don't belong here. This library is falling into a pit of hedonism with you at the helm."

"There are no take-backs. If you want to come back, I suggest you fill out an employment application for a library aid position and I'll file it in the stack with the others." I used my thumb to gesture behind me indicating the waste basket.

She stormed off and from across the room, I saw Cameron's eyes widen to saucers in surprise. I just smiled. I didn't actually want to make enemies, I just was not in any mood to take crap from anyone.

I spent the next few hours locked away in my office so I didn't go all Rambo on any of the library visitors.

"What's going on with you?"

I didn't even look up as Chyna walked in.

"Earth to my sister. Cameron said you were a 'ragin' Cajun' this morning. Did something happen between you and that sexy dragon of yours?"

I covered my face with my hands and groaned. Along with a healthy dose of embarrassment was a wild, irrational anger that my sister was a threat. She'd used the word sexy. Did she find Cezar sexy?

"You okay?"

I shook my head. "I think I'm losing my shit."

"Talk to me. I have an hour before I need to be at the diner." She grinned. "I'm meeting a date there."

I forced a smile and felt the anger dissipate. "Anyone I know?"

"Not a sexy dragon, unfortunately. Just a guy who works at the college with me." She waved her hand dismissively. "Anyway, talk to me. What's going on with your man."

"He's not my man." Or was he? "I mean, I don't think he is."

"Honey, I saw the way he looked at you. He's your man."

"It's complicated."

"It's *complicated*? What are you, a Facebook status? What's so complicated? He tells you he wants to date you. He sends you towering piles of gifts. He gives you hot orgasms. Then, even though he clearly doesn't want to, he backs off when you insist on needing *space*. What more is it gonna take for you?" She sat down on the edge of my desk and started rifling through one of the shifter books I had piled on the corner of it. "If you don't marry him or whatever it is dragons do with their women, you really have lost your shit."

Ugh, she had a point. He had done all those things even though I hadn't given him an ounce of encouragement. What did I want from him? Maybe irrefutable proof that as soon as I opened my heart to him, he wouldn't end up breaking it? Even I knew that was unreasonable to demand. I guessed I wanted what Sky had described.

"I think I need to talk to Sky."

"What? Am I not good enough? Why, because I'm a virgin and don't know any dragons besides your man?" She winked. "Kidding. Call her."

I sighed. "I hate you. You know that?"

"Mm-hmm. I love you, too. Call me tomorrow."

I watched her leave and then picked up the slip of paper with Sky's number on it. Chyna was right. I needed some advice. I only let it ring once before I was having second thoughts. On the second ring, I was just about to hang up when she answered, out of breath. "Hello?"

"Hi. This is Cherry...Cezar's...uh, friend."

"Oh! Hi, Cherry! I'm so glad you called. Is everything okay?"

"Um, yes. Everything is fine. I'm sorry if I caught you at a bad time. I can call back later."

"No, no. I was just flying with Beast. He dropped me off to go to a meeting with the others. For a bunch of dragons who say they aren't close, they sure do meet a lot." She sighed. "I wish you were catching me at a bad time. I don't know if you've flown with Cezar yet, but it's kind of the hottest thing ever."

I laughed, feeling easier. "I can agree with you there."

She cheered. "Hey, are you busy? You and I could do something, you know, have a meeting of our own. You could come over to our place and we could have dinner."

"Oh, no, I wouldn't want—"

"Great! It's a date."

"Well, but—"

"I can't wait! Our castle is only accessible by boat, so if you can meet me at the Bulcon Bay peninsula, I'll pick you up there. You know the place?"

"Well, yeah, I know—"

"Great. I'll see you soon!" She hung up, sounding way too happy with herself.

I grimaced. That hadn't gone exactly as I'd hoped it would. But, on the other hand, spending time with Sky might be just what I needed to get my thoughts straight. Maybe I could find some of the answers to all the questions in my head.

19

CEZAR

I needed my mate at my side so much that it had become physically painful to be near but unable to touch her and speak to her and caress her soft skin. I'd left my position atop the roof of the library to fly to the barge to meet the other dragon males. I'd called the meeting in the hope that perhaps they might be of assistance. I only knew I needed help.

Beast landed just before me and we shifted at the same time. He looked me over and frowned. "What's happened to you? You look like turds."

Armand landed and shifted. "He's not wrong. You look seconds from bursting into tears like a whiny youngling."

"I don't cry." I did feel like I could set the whole town aflame, though, and without much further provocation.

"What is the problem?" Beast leaned against the edge of the barge and crossed his arms over his chest. "I hope it is of significance. I had to leave my female for this."

"I found my mate." I pushed out the rest of the words before they could start congratulating me. "She rejects me."

Beast groaned. "Not this again."

Ovide landed. "What again?"

"These human women should beg us to mate them." Armand shook his head. "Don't they know we are the most superior creature that exists on this frail planet?" He crossed his arms over his wide chest. "In the old world, a female would be on her knees begging for a mating."

"That attitude might explain why you haven't found your mate yet, Ovide." Beast looked at me sympathetically. "What is the deal?"

As Remy and Blaise landed, they playfully shoved one another. Remy hissed fire at his twin and then leapt out of the way as Blaise returned flames.

I ignored them and spoke on. "I do not know. She forced me to return her to her dwelling and she refused to allow me to remain with her. She then told me that she needed *space*."

"Did you claim her? Mark her as yours?"

"No. I did show her my dragon, though. She rode on my back…"

"Did you make her wear your harness?" Armand asked with a smirk.

"No, bareback." I grinned as I said it, but then my thoughts turned serious again. "I have made considerable efforts to behave for her in ways that are comfortable to a human, but I may not be doing it right."

Beast frowned. "Sky said I came on too strong and too demanding in the beginning."

"Yes, we all remember how miserable you were. That was what I was trying to avoid. I have continued to lie low for a week and give her this *space* that she talked about."

Remy growled. "Is that what we must do for mates? Lower ourselves, crawl on our bellies like cowards?"

I threw my hands up. "I do not know. I do not want to."

"I won't do that with my mate. She will have to deal with me as a dragon. Things are the way they are."

"Spoken like a dragon with no mate and no prospects." Beast shrugged and patted me on the shoulder. "It will work out. Fate has destined this pairing."

I wanted to believe that, but I felt like Cherry was the type of woman who would fight fate. Nevertheless, I nodded and forced a smile. "I am at a low point, my friends. However, it can only go up from here."

"Speaking of up…if this is the only thing we needed to talk about, I have a date." Armand chuckled when we all swung our heads in his direction so fast a couple of us barely avoided whiplash. "With a new brew recipe! It will have the flavor of the pear." That brought us all too much joy. We all agreed that the fruit called pear was the most delicious fruit of this world.

Slowly, one by one, everyone left, until only Beast and I remained. I looked over at him and sighed. "I am worried. I am afraid that despite giving this my best effort, I am going to fail."

Fire Breathing Cezar

"My friend you are trying to behave so much like you believe a modern human male acts for a human female. Perhaps you should try being yourself."

"In case you haven't noticed, *myself* is a fire breathing brute with an overwhelming impulse to seize and conquer, to take what he desires, and I want nothing more than to toss her over my shoulder and carry her off to my castle where I will claim her as mine—mount her over and over until she is covered in my scent and fully inseminated with my seed. Not to run around like a firemouthed coward giving *space* and standing feebly as she flirts with others."

"There is a medium ground, surely. Look at me and Sky."

I nodded. "Perhaps."

"It is worth figuring out. Once you do, you shall be the happiest dragon in all the land and all that squishy mushy stuff." He made a face like he was grossed out, but I knew he was serious. Even we fire breathing beasts could be romantics.

"Are things still good with you and Sky?"

Beast's grin spread across his face so wide I thought it would crack his jaw. "She is teaching me to cook."

I nodded. "How many stoves have you gone through?"

"Five. I had to find an appliance store in the neighboring parish. Sky was getting embarrassed we had purchased so many."

"Only in this weird new world would people embarrass you about purchasing something. In the old world, we minded our business."

"Watch it, brother. You almost sound wistful about the old world. You, a modern man of this new world."

I huffed a puff of fire at him and shifted before taking off. I didn't miss the old world, not really. The times we lived in had been brutal and intense, even for kings like us. The hunters had killed so many of us before we'd left. I liked being in the new world, living without fear of a slayer's sword.

Perhaps Beast's advice was correct. Perhaps it was time to show my mate who Cezar truly was.

20

CHERRY

I hurried home to get changed into something nice for a dinner and ended up in a pair of my best dress jeans with ankle boots and a sweater. I figured it was suitable attire to be travelling through the swamp in a boat. I added a cute, trendy jacket. I told myself I wasn't dressing up on the off chance I'd run into Cezar. I just wanted to look presentable for a get together with a new friend. *Right.*

I drove myself to the designated pick-up spot, a secluded bayou peninsula a few miles south, and was just stepping out of my seven year old Honda Accord when I saw a mud boat pull up to the rickety, old wooden dock. Sky was waving me over like a mad woman.

By the look on her face, I had a sneaking suspicion she had something on her mind. Once I stepped in and got myself situated in the boat, I found out my hunch was correct.

"I have good news or I have bad news." Sky spoke without meeting my eyes, instead pretending to busy herself with the rudder and getting us on our way.

I groaned in response, but didn't say anything so she continued.

"Cezar may show up for dinner."

My heart started to flutter with a mix of fear and excitement. "Is that the good news or the bad news?"

"Both. Or either. Depending on how you take it." She held up her hands in front of her. "But I want you to know, I'm not the one who invited him, and I had nothing to do with him finding out you were coming."

I narrowed my eyes. "How else would he know?"

"It seems he's been keeping tabs on you and he knows that right now you're not at the library or at your house, so he was kinda freaking out, and, well, I told Beast that we were having a girls' get together...and Beast felt he had to tell Cezar. For the safety of the town."

"The safety of the town?"

She nodded her head emphatically as she maneuvered us around fallen logs and through dense vegetation. "When a dragon freaks out, whole cities can be reduced to rubble."

"What do you mean he's been keeping tabs on me? Keeping tabs how?"

"From what I understand, you told him you needed space?" She raised her brows questioningly. When I nodded, she continued. "Well, chère, dragons don't do space, especially a dragon whose mate is still unclaimed. Seems he's remained near you the whole time, hanging out on the library roof, the roof of your house, secretly following you wherever you went. He only left for the dragon meeting, when he returned and found you were gone..."

My jaw dropped in shock. Here, I'd been accusing him of not wanting to be around me and he'd been nearby the entire time—watching me. In the battle I'd been hosting between pain and shame, shame had suddenly emerged the clear victor. I'd been horrible to man. I told him to leave me alone, then berated him for *wanting* to leave me alone. Yet, he hadn't wanted to at all. I palmed my forehead. Could I be any more of a bitch?

To Sky's credit, she was quiet the rest of the trip, allowing me to absorb the impact of that particular piece of information.

We travelled quietly through murky waters while I stared up at the moss hanging in ropes from the thick canopy of Cypress branches above until eventually the narrower waterway opened up to a lake. Ahead I could see a dock out in front of a huge mansion. Castle, Sky had called it. Sheesh, *dragons*.

Just as we pulled up to the dock, A huge, green dragon came swooping in. Sky and I climbed out of the boat and onto the dock and as I stood stunned, unsure how to act or what to say, Sky hurried off toward the castle mumbling something about needing to check on dinner.

When Cezar transformed from amazing dragon to gorgeous naked man, I tried my best to keep from looking at his man parts. He strolled up to me like a predator stalking its prey and stopped only when he was standing toe to toe with me. My heart beat a feverish rhythm behind my ribcage and the warm, spicy, male scent of him made my thoughts fuzzy, but I held my head up and met his gaze.

I waited for him to say something, and when I couldn't wait any longer, I blurted out, "I made a mistake." And, while I still had the courage to say my piece, I figured I might as well say it all. "I shouldn't have told you I needed space. And, I shouldn't have pretended to flirt with Gary."

When I said Gary, Cezar's eyes started to glow, gold veins appeared beneath his skin and he released a low, menacing growl.

"Okay, okay! We won't mention that name. Anyway, I shouldn't have gotten mad at you for staying away when I was the one who told you to go. I just...I guess I thought that by listening to me and not staying and fighting, you didn't care. I thought you just walked away without looking back."

His hands found my waist and he pulled me even closer, letting me feel his hard length against my stomach. "I will never walk away. I will never not care. You asked me to give you space. I studied human behavior. I read that human females just want males to listen to them. I listened. I was trying to behave as a human male would—for you. I was hoping that being absent would turn your heart to fodder, or however that human saying goes."

I fought a smile. "Fonder. Absence makes the heart grow fonder."

"And did it, Cherry?" He stroked my cheek. "Did it make your heart grow fonder of me?"

The thing about sudden bursts of strength is that they aren't promised to last. After boldly speaking from my heart, honestly and openly, I wilted back to who I really was, a basket case of issues and insecurities with a bone deep acceptance of what I'd always been told about myself—that I wasn't good enough to deserve love. So, while my heart had warm fuzzies about Cezar, the rest of me was ice cold with fear and self-doubt. If thinking he'd walked away without looking back had hurt as much as it had, what would it feel like after I'd allowed myself to keep falling for him? Because with Cezar, if I didn't pull the brakes right then, I was really and truly headed for a freefall.

"Nope." I shamefully reverted to my cowardice. But, as I turned to walk away, Cezar caught my arm and swung me back into his chest. I gasped when I saw the ferocious look in his eyes. I remembered that Nick had said something about fierce, battle-hardened warriors. That was certainly the vibe I was getting at that moment.

Suddenly, his mouth descended on mine and he kissed me hard, bruising my lips with the intensity and drawing it out until I panted against his chest when he finally let me go. "Then, I am done with your human way. I am *not* human. I am a dragon and you are my female. *Mine*. There will be no more running from me. I will not allow it. You are my mate. You will accept this or see first-hand that dragons are much better at plundering than tiptoeing. There will be no more *space*."

And there it was. The defining moment of my life. The moment when everything turned on a dime. I had pushed him away, I had asked him to go, I had treated him worse than I'd probably ever treated anyone, yet he wanted—no, he was demanding—to keep me.

And, I burst into tears.

A life-time of pent-up emotion flowed down my cheeks and dripped off in salty little droplets that plopped onto the dock.

There went a teardrop of fear—buh-bye.

A teardrop of self-doubt—buh-bye.

A teardrop of unworthiness—buh-bye.

Twenty-nine years of insecurities washing away in the arms of the man who refused to let me go. I realized that it wasn't even about being good enough or not being good enough. It was about finding my person. My *dragon*. And, it wasn't only words with him. His actions backed up every sweet thing he said to me.

"My Cherry I do not mean to hurt you. You are my everything." He spoke gently as he pulled me tighter against his still naked body.

I sniffled. "You didn't hurt me. You gave me what I always wanted." I laughed as I wiped the tears from my cheeks. "And, I didn't even know I wanted it."

He held my head between his warm hands and planted kissed on my forehead, along my temples, cheeks, down to my neck.

"We could skip dinner. I prefer to be alone with you, Cherry."

I swayed. I was on the verge of saying yes and running off with him—or flying off—when Sky's voice called down from the house.

"Come on, you two! Dinner is ready!"

Fire Breathing Cezar

Cezar ran kisses down my neck. "We could pretend we didn't hear her."

I shuddered at the sensation when his lips brushed base of my throat. That was sooo tempting. "She was really nice to invite me. Besides, I suppose I need to make some friends who I can discuss this whole dragon mating thing with."

He flashed a handsome grin. Then, he looked down at his body. "You go. I must wait for Beast to bring me some clothes."

I looked, too, and licked my lips.

"C'mon" Sky called again. With one last look at his naked body, I turned and hurried up the dock towards the doorway where Sky stood. I was a new woman on a new page—one with adventure, and romance galore and I was anxious to discover what the rest of the book held for me.

I couldn't help but glance back over my shoulder with a couple parting thoughts.

21

CEZAR

Your cock looks beautiful, exposed like that.

I jumped in surprise, hearing Cherry's voice in my head as clear as day. We should not have been able to communicate like that, not yet. I had not even claimed her properly. It did not make sense. Yet, there her sweet voice was again.

I want to kneel on that dock and take you into my mouth.

I turned my back to the house, not wanting to flash anyone the massive hardon that had just sprung back up. I closed my eyes and envisioned her. *I'm still standing here. Want to come back?*

You heard me?

I heard you.

Beast's footfalls echoed down the dock and I took a few deep breaths willing myself to calm down. When I inhaled deeply, I scented Cherry's arousal. *Fuck*. I jumped into the cold lake and hoped it would help cool me down.

Just so you know, Cezar, your little mate isn't just projecting into your head. It was Beast this time.

I froze. *What?*

She's projecting into every dragon's head. It was Armand that time.

Then, Remy. *That's right. All of us.*

I was out of the lake and charging up to the house as fast as my legs could carry me. Beast threw pants at me as I passed and I almost stumbled and fell on my face trying to step into them and continue running at the same time.

I found Cherry in the kitchen with Sky, and came up behind her wrapping my arms around her waist. "So, little mate, we're going to have to work on where you're projecting all those sexy thoughts of yours."

She whipped around and stared up at me wide-eyed. "What do you mean?"

"You didn't just send that to me, apparently."

"What?!"

I held her tighter. "Just the other dragons. It's okay."

"How *many* other dragons?!" Her question was more of a shriek than a sentence. "Oh, hell, what does that even matter? One more than you is one too many!"

I agreed. "We shall work on it. Your mind is very strong. I did not even know a human could do that."

Her face was bright red. I gave her a kiss meant to comfort and calm her, but the kiss turned into more as we explored and tasted one another. Our tongues danced together and I squeezed her closer. Both of us forgot where we were until we heard a throat being cleared. Sky stood with her arms across her chest grinning.

"Go on, you two. Dinner is postponed until further notice. Get out of here and enjoy some time alone."

Cherry looked apologetic. "You sure? I mean I hate to just—"

"Oh, believe me. I'm sure. We totally get it." The heated look she and Beast exchanged confirmed it. They probably wanted to be alone, too.

I wasted no more time. All I wanted to do was get Cherry home so I could show her that I meant every word when I spoke of plundering and taking what's mine.

～

It was dark by the time we arrived at my castle. As soon as I changed back from my dragon form, I insisted on carrying Cherry over the threshold. I had read it was a human custom, and although I was finished behaving as a human, I wanted to assure her that I still honored her.

She enjoyed it and laughed as I continued to carry her up the spiral staircase to my bedchamber. Cherry's eyes went wide as she scanned the room and I hoped she liked it. I wanted her to come and live with me in my castle, but if it was not to her satisfaction, I would tear it down and build another for her.

I sat her down on the edge of the bed and stood between her thighs. I flipped the button on her jeans and as she lifted up, I slid them slowly down her smooth thighs. I knelt in front of her and stared at the contrast of her white panties against her silky brown skin as my fingers tightened on her hips. I fought to control my dragon.

"Cezar... You're glowing." Her voice was breathy, her hands soft as she brushed them over my face.

I could feel my dragon at the surface, begging to take her. I knew my body looked different when I was so close to shifting, but I couldn't pull away. "I want you so bad, Cherry. Every night, I have to stroke myself to relieve some of the tension. I think of you, kneeling in front of me, taking me into your hot mouth."

She gasped and her thighs opened the slightest bit more. "You do?"

I kissed her inner thigh and looked up at her. "I do. I think about being in you, the way your sweet little body grips me and sucks me in deeper, about the way you look when you come. I can't stop thinking about that."

"I think about you, too." The admission made her cheeks turn a darker shade, and I loved the way her eyes hooded as she met my gaze.

I hooked my thumbs in the band of her panties and slowly pulled them down and off. I spread her even farther apart and took in the sight of her. She was stunning. With her sex on display to me, I felt like a god. I could see her arousal wetting her folds and I knew that I'd done that. She was as turned on by me as I was by her.

I lowered my face and ran my tongue over her folds, tasting her. She trembled and braced herself on her hands behind her.

I wrapped my arms around her thighs and pulled her into my face, supporting her and controlling her at the same time. When I buried my mouth into her, she let out a naughty little yelp that told me she wasn't far from coming already. I knew that would simply be the first of many that night and that I would not stop until she had multiple orgasms. I wanted her to be, what was the human phrase? Thoroughly fucked.

Cherry was not silent. She screamed her orgasm, encouraging me with her cries so much that I did not cease until she had come again and again and begged me to stop because she needed a rest. I could have feasted on my mate for days and not gotten tired of it. She was sweet and delicious and I'd never get enough of her.

As she worked to regain her breath, I stood and pulled her into my arms, cradling her. Pressing my lips to her ear, I told her how I felt. "This dragon should've been smart enough to tell you that you are his mate from the start. I am sorry I hurt you, but I will make it up to you. No matter how long it takes."

We made love well into the night until Cherry was exhausted and fell sound asleep. There would be time to claim her, but despite the fact that I was no longer behaving the way I thought human males might, I would not do it before explaining to her what it meant. It had to be her choice. As she slumbered deeply, I snuggled her against me on my bed and spent the rest of the night watching her as she slept.

22

CHERRY

It was dead quiet on that Saturday morning. The kids who'd come to audition for the Christmas play had gone and the library was empty. Cameron had called in sick and I didn't think there was another person in the whole place. I walked around to make sure and found no one.

It was almost noon—closing time on Saturdays. I decided that I'd close up early and go home. Cezar had been hanging around all morning, so I figured he was outside somewhere. But, when I locked the front doors and looked around for him, I didn't see him. I even stepped back and tried to see on the roof. Not there.

I shouldn't have panicked. I knew he wouldn't have gone far but I supposed old habits were hard to break and old insecurities rose up from time to time.

I know I'm sending this to all of you dragons, but just turn your hearing off, or something. I'm just trying to talk to Cezar. Where are you, my dragon?

Minutes passed and I still didn't see or hear from Cezar. I was getting annoyed, and worried. If Cezar didn't show up soon, I was going to hide in my house and eat a half gallon of cookie dough ice cream.

I headed towards home with no pep in my step. Had I done something to push Cezar away?

The closer I got to my house, the more I didn't want to be there. I considered calling out to him again, but I didn't want all of the dragons around to know how desperate I was.

Defeated, I carted my sad self in and dropped my bag just inside the door. Heading towards the kitchen, I had a date with a bucket of ice cream. I'd barely made it into the kitchen when I was grabbed from behind. I screamed, but then a rough hand was over my mouth and a firm body was pressed up behind me. I knew instantly it was Cezar.

"Is this what you want, little mate? You want the dragon?" His voice was rough in my ear and his teeth weren't any gentler as they scraped along my skin. "Do you know how dragons used to claim their dragon females?"

I shivered. "No."

"They just took what they wanted. They'd come up to their mate and sink their teeth into her neck, marking her as their own before they even so much as said hello. Then, with their teeth still in her neck, they'd lift her skirt and thrust their cock inside of her. Is that what you want?"

I moaned, helpless to the eroticism of Cezar's words and his husky voice. His cock was snuggly trapped against my ass and he rocked into me as she spoke.

"Do you want to see how badly I need you? Do you want to be taken and fucked while I mark you, my Cherry?

"I will sink my teeth into your neck and let your blood flow into me. While I'm fucking you. That mark? It will bind us together forever. You will stop aging, you will be with me until the day we both die, thousands of years from now. Do you understand that?"

I jerked my head roughly. Sky had explained it to me, and not only was I a hundred percent onboard, I found the whole thing erotic as hell.

"Is that what you want?"

I felt his hesitation to my very soul. He wasn't sure I'd say yes. He actually thought I might reject him again. It struck me as odd that we were both self-conscious in that way. Him, a two-hundred-ton warrior dragon, and me, a bookish librarian with difficult hair.

I fought against his hold, but it was like trying to flick through concrete with a pinky finger. "Dammit, Cezar, yes!"

He froze against my back. "Yes?"

"Yes! Hell yes! That's what I want. Wow, and you thought I needed to be cared for the way a human male would do it?"

"I…"

"Because I think I'm much more suited to be the mate of a dragon. Which is probably why fate matched us in the first place. Because I need a possessive beast like you."

We were both breathing roughly against each other, the mood between us dangerous. Cezar growled lower. "You did not seem pleased when I tried to show my affection."

I cleared my throat. "I didn't think it was real. How could someone who looks like you be into someone like me?"

"How—you're the most beautiful woman I've ever seen. And, you could have just asked me."

"And what would you have said?" I threw his words back at him.

"I would've said that I wanted you, human. You. No one else. Fate made you for me. The worlds knew what I would want and they gave me you." He lightly pushed me away. "They knew that my perfect mate would be someone who needed me to fight for her, to work for the honor of claiming her. I don't think I've earned it yet, Cherry."

I licked my lips. "What do you mean?"

"You want a dragon." He gave me a wicked grin. "You got a dragon."

My pulse kicked into high gear. "What does that mean, Cezar?"

"It means you should run. When I catch you, there's no stopping, little mate."

The urge to run took over and I charged away from him. Up the stairs, two at a time, I fled into my bedroom and slammed the door shut. Then, into the bathroom. My heart raced. I could feel how aroused I was already. It made no sense, but nothing about being with Cezar did. He was a dragon, for god sakes.

"Where are you, little mate?" He came up the stairs slowly and so sure of himself.

A thrill shot through me and I decided to really make him work for me. I shoved open the bathroom window and climbed out of it. The roof was gently sloped, enough for me to move down it and shimmy down the drain pipe at the side of my house. What I was doing literally made no sense, but my body seemed to recognize the game I was playing with Cezar's dragon. I somehow knew that the chase would make the catch even better.

As crazy as the whole thing sounded, it felt right. So, I ran. Down the street, around the library and up the fire escape in the back. By the time I got to the top, I was out of breath and bouncing on the balls of my feet. I knew he'd be there soon.

Ready or not, dragon, here I am.

23

CEZAR

I'd never felt like so much of my dragon come through without actually changing forms. I lifted my nose to the night sky and inhaled. Following Cherry's scent wasn't hard. I knew where she was as soon as I hit the street. Still, I took my time getting there. I could smell her thrill and arousal in the air and I was becoming drunk on it. I walked calmly down the street and behind the library. When my hand connected with the metal ladder to climb to the roof, I heard clearly her intake of breath.

Don't be scared now, little mate.

"I'm not scared! I'm bored. Sometime tonight, would you?"

I laughed and scaled the ladder in seconds. At the top, Cherry had been leaning over to see me. She jumped back and licked her lips. I prowled towards her, feeling the mating call through my entire body.

"How'd you do that?"

I grinned at her. "Magic. Want to see more magic?"

She laughed while backing away. "Is this the part where you pull down your pants to reveal your magic wand?"

"This is the part where I back you up until you're sitting on the edge of this roof and then I fuck you like you desperately want to be fucked." I stepped closer to her and watched as she naturally took a big step back. "Scared?"

"In your dreams."

"Then why are you backing away?"

"I'm not."

I raised an eyebrow and closed the gap between us. The back of her knees pressed into the brick ledge and she fell onto her butt.

Take off your dress, Cherry. I need to see you.

She stood up and met my gaze. Shoving her jacket off, she made quick work of the dress until she was standing in just her underwear and boots, she was the most exquisite beauty that ever lived. "Your turn."

I ripped my clothes off and then extended a talon to easily cut through her bra and panties. I wanted her naked. *Better*.

"Tell me more about what you would've done differently."

"I'll tell you what I should've done." I pressed her body into mine and groaned at the feel of her puckered nipples raking over my chest. "When I saw you that first day, I should've followed you into that hallway of books you were hiding in. I should've grabbed you by the back of your neck and pulled you into me.

"I should've reached down your pants while kissing you and fucked you with my fingers until I knew you were ready for me." I trailed my hand down her body and slipped my fingers into her wet folds. Two of my fingers easily slid into her. "Then, I should have held your head to the side to expose the tender skin of your neck and sank my teeth into your lovely mocha flesh."

When I pretended to do just that, she gasped and her core pulsed around my fingers. As soon as she realized I hadn't actually marked her, she slapped my arm. "Don't tease."

"You are nervous?"

"Sky told me it didn't hurt."

"I mean about being tethered to me forever."

She wrapped her arms around my neck and moaned when I curled my fingers and hit that special spot inside of her. "No."

I lifted her into my arms and pulled my fingers out of her, just to slid into her with my cock. I growled at the sensation of her tight sheath gripping me while she tossed her head back and moaned. Her neck was exposed and my dragon urged me to take her, claim her with my mark. As much as I wanted to, though, I wanted her to be so ready for it that she'd beg.

I turned us around and sat on the ledge. Cherry immediately settled in and rocked against my lap. I grabbed her ass and moved her body faster. I wanted her to lose control. I filled her hard and fast, my body stroking her clit as we moved back and forth.

Her nails scored my back, the way they always did, and her mouth came down to mine. She bit my lower lip and then sucked it into her mouth to soothe it. Kissing down to my neck, she bit me there, leaving her own mark. She gave just as rough as she got.

I could feel my dragon rising to the surface and fought back the urge to let go. Rocking our bodies together, I felt her start to come apart. Her body tightened around me, her nails dug deeper. Her bites turned to sweet little nips as the pleasure she felt distracted her.

Come for me, little mate. I want to feel you shatter.

Cherry tossed her head back and let out a wild scream that only got louder when I sank into her once more before plunging my teeth into her neck. I came harder than I'd ever come in my life, each jerk thrashing my body like it was coming from the deepest part of my soul. Cherry's body squeezed mine hard as her voice broke and her scream cut short. She collapsed in my arms, my teeth still in her neck.

I held her tight against my chest and I slowly licked at the drops of blood spilled there. It was like a sweet elixir, luring me closer to her. Crushing her to me, I whispered in her ear what she meant to me. Everything.

Mate, sweet mate.

"Cezar…"

I stroked her back and waited to talk until we both came down from the high. Both of our bodies still trembled against each other, the magnitude of what we'd just done not lost on us.

"That was...insane." She rested her forehead on my shoulder and blew out a breath. "What the hell just happened?"

Magic.

"You broke into my house like some kind of crazy person and then somehow we ended up on a roof... Is it always like this?"

"Sometimes, we'll use a bed."

She grinned. "I...we're together now?"

"Yes."

"So, you're my boyfriend?"

I shifted. "I'm a little bit more than that."

"My fiancé?"

"Um, did you not understand what—"

She laughed and kissed the end of my nose, jumpstarting my body again. "I'm teasing you. I know. We're together forever."

Not nice.

"Will you teach me how to not talk to everyone over the dragon party line?"

"I could. But I kind of like it when everyone knows how pretty you think my cock looks."

Oh, Cezar, don't worry about not being able to get it up. It's not a big deal.

"Hey!"

She laughed and wiggled on my lap. "I could get used to this."

"You're going to have to." I caught her face in my hand and kissed her gently. "You're stuck with me. Forever."

"I need to ask a favor.

"Anything."

"I want you to help me find my sister a dragon mate."

I blinked. "What?"

"You heard me. If I'm living for thousands of years, so is she."

EPILOGUE
CHERRY

I was so busy with Cezar that I forgot all about my sister and worrying about finding her a mate. The sex drive that came along with having a dragon mate was unbelievable. I had never been all that interested in sex before, and I figured that whenever I did finally lose my virginity, my taste would be very vanilla. Turns out that it wasn't just my soul that had been waiting for a connection. My body had also been waiting for a hunky dragon to come along before it flipped its libido switch. I could barely keep my hands off of Cezar long enough to get anything done. And, when I was able to resist, he wasn't.

At work, I longed for him. At home, I indulged in him. During the night, I woke up tangled in him, sometimes with each of us already halfway to orgasm. Like that Aretha Franklin song *(You Make Me Feel Like A) Natural Woman*, he made me feel like a wanton seductress instead of a boring, plump, almost-but-not-quite-pretty librarian. Some days I was dead tired and running on fumes, but still I wanted sex with my dragon.

When I started feeling queasy in the mornings, it didn't take me long to figure it out. Tender breasts. Nausea. Oodles of unprotected sex. One trip to the drugstore and eight dollars later, what I knew to be true was confirmed. I was knocked up.

Cezar and I hadn't yet talked about children. I hadn't even thought about whether or not our two species could even produce offspring. I guess that was a question that was answered before it was asked.

Whoa, Nelly. Was I pregnant with a *dragon*?

It was about that time that I started to seriously panic. Cezar wasn't an alien per se, well, not the abducting and taking me back to his planet to be an enslaved breeder kind of alien, but he was a different type of creature. And he'd gotten me pregnant. How would I carry a dragon baby?

I had so many questions and the only dragons I knew were men. What good would they be? I'd have to have a home birth. I couldn't exactly give birth to a dragon in a hospital. What if my baby was born in dragon form? Would it enter the world with wings? Oh, sweet baby Jesus, would I lay an egg?

Cezar walked in on me hyperventilating while also trying to Google anything I could on dragon births. Of course, there was nothing to find so I had to improvise but for the life of me, I couldn't figure out if dragons were reptiles or amphibians. Was Cezar more crocodile or alligator? Actually, neither, he was more like those giant prehistoric birds, the pterodactyls.

"What are you doing? Calm down, Cherry. What's wrong?"

He stroked my hair and back, obviously not aware that I had a damned good reason to panic.

"I never wanted natural childbirth at home. I wanted a hospital, with lots of drugs and nurses and doctors. I don't tolerate pain well, Cezar!"

He frowned. "Little mate, what are you talking about?"

"You knocked me up! I'm pregnant and gonna have a giant prehistoric *bird*!"

"What?!" Cezar shouted and stepped back. "What? You're pregnant?!"

I gestured to my body as though he should've been able to see it. "Look at me! There's an egg in there!"

"Okay, stop calling it a bird. Dragons are not birds, Cherry." He knelt in front of me and pressed his head to my belly. "We made a youngling?"

"Am I going to die? How am I going to give birth to a giant dragon egg?"

"Our young will not be in dragon form when you birth him...or her. And he or she will definitely not be an egg." He looked up at me with stars in his eyes. "We're having a youngling!"

"You didn't answer my question. Am I going to die in childbirth?"

"No! You're not going to die. I watched that *Alien* movie you were talking about and it's disgusting. You really think I'm some awful creature like that?"

Fire Breathing Cezar

Well, when he put it like that. I took a few calming breaths and shrugged. "Sometimes, you're a monster."

He laughed and pulled me onto the floor with him. "You think so? You think I am a monster?"

I slapped his hands away when he tried to tickle me, but he held both of my arms down with one hand and tickled me with the other. "Don't make me laugh! This is serious!"

"Monsters *are* serious business! Do not dare laugh!" He pulled my shirt up and blew a raspberry on my stomach. "Our youngling's first memory."

Despite myself, I found that I was laughing with him and suddenly thinking about what he would be like as a father. Amazing, without a doubt. Just like he'd proven to be an amazing mate. Generous and kind, he gave me what I needed, when I needed it. He had even learned how to calm me down when I started to, as Chyna said, "overdramatize things."

"You're going to be the very best mother, Cherry."

"I hope so. I didn't get much of an example of that the way I grew up."

He wrapped me in his arms and pulled me on top of him. "I did not have an example of a good father, either. That doesn't matter, though. We can give our young everything we did not have."

"We're going to have a baby."

"Shall we tell the others since you haven't been able to stop projecting your thoughts to everyone yet?" He grunted when I elbowed him in the stomach.

Cezar, you really have to stop beating yourself up about your small...problems.

"And you call me a monster. Listen to yourself." Cezar rolled us over so that he was on top of me. "I should spank your bottom. That would teach you."

I smiled a smile that came from deep in my heart because there was no other place in the world I'd rather be and no other person I'd rather be with. I'd found *home* and I knew that I didn't have to worry about courting heartache. I didn't have to worry about courting anything other than my big, handsome dragon shifter.

I projected again. *Hey, guys. We're having a baby.*

Cezar grinned. *Or a large bird egg. My Cherry has not decided yet.*

I laughed. "This means war, mister."

I screamed when he brandished his long teeth at me and jumped to his feet, looming over me. "Cezar, no!"

He squatted in an attack position. "Better run, little human. The big, dragon monster is coming for you."

I flew to my feet and out of the room, Cezar right on my heels. I was never able to get very far away from him, but it didn't matter. The chase was a game we both loved and it never failed to end in a series of rapturous, explosive orgasms for the both of us.

How strange life was. All I had wanted was to turn a new page in my life. That was the thing I loved about books, though, you never knew what was gonna happen on the next page. Who knew my new page would reveal adventure and romance to rival the wildest adventure book in my beloved library?

"Slow down, Cezar! You're chasing too fast!"

"Have you become slower already? How will you ever escape me sinking my teeth into that sweet flesh of yours, little mate?"

As though I wanted to.

Next Book:
Fire Breathing Blaise

Printed in Great Britain
by Amazon